D1462053

EXILE ON VLAHIL

By Ardath Mayhar

EXILE
ON
VLAHIL

ARDATH MAYHAR

DOUBLEDAY & COMPANY, INC.

GARDEN CITY, NEW YORK

1984

All of the characters in this book are fictitious,
and any resemblance to actual persons,
living or dead,
is purely coincidental.

Library of Congress Cataloging in Publication Data

Mayhar, Ardath.
Exile on Vlahil.

I. Title.
PS3563.A962E9   1984   813'.54

ISBN: 0-385-17825-5
Library of Congress Catalog Card Number 82-45300
Copyright © 1984 by ARDATH MAYHAR
All Rights Reserved
Printed in the United States of America

First Edition

EXILE ON VLAHIL

CHAPTER ONE

Ila shivered. The cubicle wasn't truly cold, but the chill gray of the walls, the sterile atmosphere, struck her with arctic impact.

The only furnishing meant for human use was a hard stool centered mathematically in the square of floor. She sat, and then she shivered with good cause, for the metal was icy. A click and a buzz at the console before her brought her to alertness. The blue tape that had followed her through the weeks just past was feeding into a slot in the neat rectangle of the console, and the rippling of light, clucking, chuckling, and humming began.

Ila shifted her bare buttocks on the stool, trying to settle for the usual long wait while computers consulted with slow human judges. But she was interrupted by the deep and falsely sympathetic voice she had come to hate with great sincerity.

"Ila Fazieh," it intoned, and she gritted her teeth. A sentence of death would, at the very least, deliver her from the bullying of machinery. "You have been examined at length, tried by human and computer judges, and found guilty of felony. By your own admission, you have refused mental conditioning, thereby denying this culture the full benefit of your capacities and loyalties. Your activities in opposition to the Exile Policy have placed you outside the protection of the law, and your own action has denied you readmittance. You will be exiled to a suitable planet, to be chosen by lot, there to live the rest of your life. You may ask questions."

"Are . . ." Her throat went dry, and she coughed. "Are there other alternatives?"

"No."

"Are there likely to be other human beings there?"

"The planet has not yet been programmed," the voice said with disapproval. "It cannot be said with accuracy. However, an attempt is made to distribute criminals as thinly as possible throughout the accessible galaxies. In this way, a human foothold is established in places that might not be examined for millennia. It is highly unlikely there should be other human occupants."

Ila sat silent. No question entered her mind, though she knew that this opportunity would not come again. She squirmed on the cold stool, which even her bare skin hadn't succeeded in warming. The console rippled quietly for a moment. Abruptly, the lights went out, and the humming stopped. The door zipped open behind her, and Ila rose and marched out.

A Servo met her with a gray coverall, which she donned gratefully. The most shattering aspect of her time in the hands of the legal system had been the nakedness. She could imagine that it would bring almost anyone to a shaken and amenable state. Fortunately for her, she had never attempted to deny her guilt or to avoid her sentence, though she had hoped for a lesser sentence than exile.

The Servo tugged at her arm, and she followed it automatically. To her surprise, she found herself in an interview room, where her father waited, his face gray with worry as he rose to hug her.

In that warm haven, Ila closed her eyes for a moment, trying to recapture the secure composure of her childhood. Then she stepped back and took his brown hands in hers.

"I didn't know they ever let anyone in here, Pup," she said. "Who got his personal wealth enhanced? And how do you go about bribing a Servo?"

Ralph Fazieh smiled, his deeply olive face wrinkling into fine lines, but the pain in his eyes didn't fade. "There are ways, my dear. There are many ways for getting where you must . . . and putting things where you need for them to be. They will take you into the Transfer soon. You will go into Chamber 1535. On the floor in the corner will be a Companion. It is much smaller, much more complex than the one that taught you as a child. Hold it close, and it will go through with you, wherever it is they choose to send you." His face crumpled, and he turned away.

Ila put her arms about his waist and laid her cheek against his back. "Don't suffer, Pup. I asked for it, you know that. And you, too, if you think about it. It was you who told me never to let go, when I knew I was right. And you have Milla to comfort you. I won't be dead . . . and I won't, just maybe, stay furious all the time. And I won't have to battle the Instrumentality. You may wind up wishing you had gone with me."

His hands gripped hers, crushing them against the front of his tunic. "All the luck, baby," he whispered, as she felt the cold hand of the Servo again upon her elbow.

"Hold on!" she cried, as she was led away. "Don't let them bend you, Pup!" Then the door zipped shut, and he was gone.

The Transfer was tremendous. It occupied, she remembered from her anti-Exile days, a fifty-mile square and towered forty stories. From that gray building, the colonists had gone out, generations ago, to live on far planets. The explorers had passed through its chambers in their insatiable hunt for new systems, new planets, new points to mark on their charts and new facts to record in their edutapes. Five hundred years ago, the method of Transfer had been developed to the point at which anything—or anyone—could be instantly transported to any point in the galaxy that was Earth's.

A hundred years ago, the method had been further refined to include any point in any galaxy for which referents were available. And the people had gone, willingly at first, into far places where they could again feel themselves masters of their own fates. So the old Earth had been left with a fraction of its population, and the social engineers had sighed with satisfaction. Such a condition would lead, they maintained, to a near-perfect social system, in balance with the planet, uncrowded and unharassed.

Ila snorted, but the Servo only tightened its grip and hustled her from the tube-car and into the tunnel leading into the Transfer. So much for social engineers. A machine could be far more dictatorial, far more cold-blooded than the worst human being. And machines had no patience with the erratic, the creative, or the stubborn. "Lord knows, I'm all of those," she said to the Servo, which, as it never listened unless waiting for an answer, was not puzzled by the remark.

Through a maze of passages, up endless lift-tubes, down numberless featureless corridors they went, pausing at last before a gray door marked 1535. The halves zipped apart, the Servo pushed, the leaves of the door whispered shut again, and Ila found herself alone in a cubicle barely wide enough to accommodate her extended arms. But in the corner, as her father had promised, there was a compact box wrapped in sheenite and tied with all-purpose rope.

Without hesitation, Ila squatted and caught the box to her chest, then rose, holding it fast to her body as she felt the world give itself a shake and a quiver. There was a timeless period of not-quite-being, and then she felt another shiver, another shaking of molecules, and she stood . . . elsewhere.

There was a sun above, somewhat smaller, it seemed to her, than the one she knew. There was grassy stuff under her feet and extremely tall, narrow trees that were startlingly green. And before her stood a low, ugly, utilitarian hut that she knew had been Transferred for her use. She sighed, opened the manually operated door and stepped inside.

That voice said, above her head, "Ila Fazieh, you have been exiled to the planet Vlahil. Here there is no humanoid life form that the remote scanner could perceive, though there are many native life forms. None of them were determined to be unusually predatory. There is a weapon with batteries that may be recharged by exposure to sunlight, if any dangerous beasts should appear. It is remotely possible that other human beings may exist in this system, as a scout ship was lost in this sector some months ago.

"The air is usable without any adaptation, as is the water. A food analyzer is in the kitchen area. With it you will determine which of the natural foods is fit for your use, before the stored supply is exhausted. This shelter will last for nine Earth years, by which time you will be either dead or will have adapted sufficiently to build your own."

There was a click, and the voice was, at last, gone for good.

Ila had listened with attention, but now her mouth assumed its most skeptical twist. "I'll bet," she muttered, "your remote scanner made one fast pass at this lump of dirt and reported practically nothing of value, and your experts back on Earth dressed up the nothing they had to make it sound just fine for some poor exile." She remembered her long studies of the Exile System, some of them delving into reports and record systems not intended for the eyes of the uninitiated. The lofty purposes and ethics of the originators of the program had definitely not, she recalled, been followed to the letter.

She turned with considerably more enthusiasm to the box her father had provided. The sheenite unrolled with its accustomed ease, revealing several yards of the waterproof, acid-resistant, and lightweight material. The supple line that secured it was tied with a double half-hitch, one end disappearing into the box. Several yards were coiled within. And beside it, carefully wrapped, was the Companion, a solar-powered all-purpose computer small enough to be carried, if change of location should be necessary. Tucked into the small amount of space left were plio-packs of seeds, each labeled, with instructions for planting rolled securely inside.

She grinned. Come catastrophe, come chaos, her father was the most practical of men. With what he had provided, given anything edible that would nourish her metabolism for even a short while, she could survive . . . and keep her sanity. She thumbed the pressure switch on the side of the Companion and asked, "Do you contain the poetry of Keats?"

A schoolmarmish voice answered, "Of course;

also 'The Songs of Silence,' from *The Venusian Études,* most of the classic literature from the French, English, Sanskrit, and Greek, all the works of your favorite classical and modern composers. Your father knows your tastes, Ila. But I am programmed to aid you in analyzing alien situations, principally, and I have been altered to include a fairly comprehensive universal translator. You may talk with me as if I were another person, as I have been provided with a complete personality profile."

"Good enough," the girl said, patting the shiny black case. "We'll be two against the world, whatever world it is. Vlahil? Not even in the data lists did I ever encounter this one."

"Actually, the planet was called 1 KXT 23 by the computer at Exile Headquarters, but for some unknown reason all the humans who dealt with the records insisted on calling the place Vlahil. Independently of one another, I might add." The Companion hummed thoughtfully for a moment, then added, "It has occurred to me that the recordings of the scanner may have picked up some emanation unintelligible to computers but which reached the subconscious part of the human mind. Just a thought."

"Which might indicate some sort of intelligence . . . somewhere," mused Ila, as she reached up and tore loose the speaker from which That Voice had come and hurled it against the wall. Then, feeling much better, she turned to the kitchen corner of the shelter and peered into the bins and cabinets.

"Ugh! Some Servo with sadist tendencies must select the food." She opened a sliding section of the wall, revealing three coveralls, all gray, three pairs of boots, three pairs of sandals, packets containing what appeared to be underwear and socks, a stack of pamphlets with the symbol of the Instrumentality on their covers, and a set of basic tools—hammer, saw, hoe, level, shovel, axe, pick, and several she couldn't identify. Everything was gray except the metal.

"Is gray dye cheaper than colored?" she asked the Companion. "And is gray paint more plentiful than any other? Why in the Universe do mechanisms like gray so much?"

The Companion gave what might be construed to be a chuckle. "Actually, it isn't the cost of the paint and dye, it's the cost of the robot," she said. "Cheap Servos are color-blind, expensive ones are not. The Instrumentality prides itself on its thrift, so it uses cheap Servos in the Transfer program. They see everything as gray anyway, so gray is the only color provided them. Otherwise, you would have an orange-and-purple house with a magenta roof. It's calmer this way, actually."

"It makes sense," answered Ila, thumbing through the pamphlets. "Perish and drat! Do they send anything about contacting possible intelligent life forms? Do they send instructions on how to farm in an alien environment? Or even directions on building an emergency shelter? *Control Your Thinking for the Public Good,* egad! *The Instrumentality, a Perfect*

System of Government. The Necessity for Exile. You know, there isn't anything useful in this whole pile."

The Companion emitted something between a giggle and a click. "Don't throw it away. It *is* paper, and certain physical functions are far more satisfactory when there is paper at hand."

Ila stared hard at the black box. "Are you sure you've never been . . . well, alive?" she asked.

"I was given the entire taped persona and memory of a librarian named Alice Schuwitcz. She donated herself to science just before she died of cancer at the age of eighty-five."

Ila's eyes flashed, and she gave a little grunt of laughter. "Trust my father to do the thing properly," she chuckled. "Alice, my lass, you little thought, probably, in your hive of tapes and films and cracked old books, to share exile with a convicted rebel. What do you think of your new career?"

The slick black box muttered to itself for a moment, and the tiny light on its top flicked on and off half a dozen times in rapid succession. Then Alice's voice said, "Actually, young woman, I think we'll get along fine. I happen to be the rebel who yelled and stomped loudly enough so that the Instrumentality was forced to discard their intention of destroying all original books and manuscripts, after editing them onto tape in ways that proved whatever was useful to the Unholy I at the moment. Your history is in my files, and if I had lost a husband into the Exile System, I'd have fought them, too."

"Good enough," said Ila. "Now I'll warm some of this disgusting goo, and you can be glad you're beyond the need of it."

"I shall be happy to accompany you, in memory, by describing the finest meal I ever ate," replied Alice.

And, as the dwarfed sun moved down the sky, the two earthlings savored a long-digested repast, and Ila smiled, as she had not thought to do again, and looked out the window at the delicately toothed mountains that reared themselves above the horizon.

CHAPTER TWO

The night seemed interminable. Ila lay in her foampack, sleepless, for what must have been hours. At last she dozed, only to be awakened by something bumping with elephantine bulk into her shelter. Creeping to the transparent panel in the wall, she peered out into a chaos of shifting shadow.

Gradually, her eyes began to adjust to the strange lighting and discovered that the dome was surrounded by a multitude of creatures that seemed to be busily investigating the structure. As she watched by starlight, she grew gradually aware that the light was getting stronger. Scanning the sky as far as her field of vision would allow, she discovered a small, pale moon newly risen over the spindly mountains. The addition of its light allowed her to see her visitors more clearly, and she tallied those just beside her window.

"Something like an overgrown mouse with hands —gracious, it just blew its nose on a leaf . . . I think!

"A pig-sized thing with no features at all, just a smooth sphere with lumps for legs, which seems to be scratching its rear (or maybe nose) against the wall.

"A very large, leggy creature that seems to be trying to clasp the whole shelter to its bosom. *That* is what woke me!

"Something very much like a teddy bear with luminous ears.

"Eek! A spidery, snaky thing with arms or tentacles covered with hair. . . .

"And something that seems to be just as interested in me as I am in it . . . Alice!" And she trundled the Companion over to the window and touched the switch. "Look out there, my friend, and tell me what you think of the lumpy thing that is shaped something like a small man."

As Alice studied the creature, it drew nearer to the window. Evidently the rising moon cast enough light into the room to make their shapes visible to it, for it came up against the panel and cupped its hands about its eyes to shut out the reflections.

Alice, with her vision cells almost level with the creature's, hummed and clicked for some time. After its first quiver of surprise or fear at the flashing of her toplight, the little being showed no uneasiness as it continued looking into the room.

At last, the Companion said, "This is an intelligent life form, which is determinable by its actions. The others are animals of varying degrees of development, but this is something we should investigate. Would you rather be safe for tonight or learn something valuable at some risk? I think we should open the panel and see if I can find some basis on which to communicate with it."

Ila knelt beside Alice and looked into those darkly shaded eyes. They were just barely visible by the light reflected back into them from her moon-washed face, and their expression of deep sadness was moving. Ila rose and patted Alice's case.

"I guess we'll just invite the green-eyed monster into our parlor," she said. "If I can manage the ridiculous assortment of fastenings on this panel."

In a moment, the lower section of the window slid aside into the wall. At its motion, the creature started, then stepped back a pace to watch its disappearance. Then it moved forward and examined the edge, flush with the wall. Its eyes glittered greenly in the light that Ila activated, as it leaned into the opening, then climbed slowly through into the shelter.

"Hello," said Ila, totally lacking in small talk suitable for an alien intelligence.

Lumpy (as she had christened it) nodded its roughly molded head eagerly, came forward and laid its hand on her wrist. Its skin was mud-colored in the artificial light, and it had six strong-looking but dexterous fingers, which it immediately withdrew from her wrist and laid upon Alice.

After some humming and clicking, Alice said, "It seems to be mute, but I am getting a field of some sort from its touch. It is outside my present capacities, though I have a feeling that in the old days I would have understood something from it. I have a wild idea—try laying your hand on my case, just by

his . . . its. I can amplify the field, I think. Just clear
your mind and let it pick up what it can."

Ila stepped cautiously forward, extending her
hand slowly so the creature wouldn't take fright at
her movements. When she touched Alice's case, she
immediately felt something buzz inside her head,
growing in intensity until she said, "Hold it down,
Alice, I think it's too strong. It comes through as a
big buzz, but there are pictures, too, if I can bring
them clear."

Gradually the vibrations dimmed. "Hold right
there!" she cried to Alice at last. "Alice, old girl, we
have something here."

Inside her skull, Ila found clear pictures forming
. . . vast panoramas framed by arched stone door-
ways, with winged figures soaring and dipping in
flight that was the distilled essence of grace. Interi-
ors, seemingly lighted by brilliance inside the stone,
with walls carven into lacework and furnishings of
blown-glass delicacy. And, at work with what could
only be a chisel, a creature of the kind that stood
beside her. It was cutting a design into the lintel of a
door, tracing lines of impossible fineness into what
seemed to be granite.

She lifted her hand from the Companion and extended it timidly toward the creature by the window.
He (she knew, somehow, that the aura of its thought
was male) looked at her with glowing green eyes,
sadly, sadly, and touched her fingers with his. A
sound echoed in her mind . . . Ered, Ered, Ered.

Excitedly, she touched the translation button and

said to him, "Say something, talk to me, so the machine can find your linguistic concepts. Talk . . ." And she touched her lips, moving them in the patterns of speech, then pointed to his mouth.

The Ered laid a many-fingered hand across his lips, then waved it from side to side in a gesture of complete negation.

Ila again set her hand against his and pictured herself speaking to the Ered, and the Ered she pictured had no mouth. In return she received a picture of an Ered with no mouth but with exaggerated ears.

"Mute, but not deaf," she exclaimed to Alice. "What do we do now?"

The Companion hummed and clicked for some time. Then: "It is evidently used to communicating with a verbal race . . . it has gestures, it shows no alarm at telepathic contact. We must try to make it understand that we need to meet those who talk to it."

This time Ila, for lack of any other referent common to the two of them, visualized for the Ered a scene wherein one of the winged creatures was standing (somewhat awkwardly, for she had no clear idea of its anatomy) and talking with the Ered.

A burst of red-orange explosions filled her inner vision, accompanied by an overwhelming sense of amusement. "Ered laughs in orange sunbursts," she remarked to Alice. Then the picture reappeared, and the winged being, much taller than she had seen it, was standing easily and gracefully on its toe-tips, fluttering its wings gently to keep its weight mostly airborne. Its very thin lips were moving, and Ila felt that with just a bit of practice she could actually hear what it said. The Ered in the picture was equipped with mouth and normal Ered ears (somewhat small, but evidently acute), and it seemed to be replying occasionally with fluent, fluid gestures of the hands.

She added to the scene a figure as nearly like herself as she could make it, causing it to walk slowly toward the pair, stop, and hold out its hand to the winged one. Again, she heard interiorly a sound. "Vlammalba."

"Vlammalba," she repeated, and the Ered made a sweeping pass with his hand that said, quite clearly, "Yes."

Alice said, "Tell him we need to rest the night, but to try to bring a Vlammalba to see us tomorrow."

"If I didn't see your black case and your running light, I'd swear you were flesh and blood, Alice," said Ila. "You're a comfort, which is exactly what my father intended, no doubt."

She turned again to the Ered and made a picture of the darkened shelter, of herself asleep in the bedpack. Then she showed the Ered returning in daylight, leading a Vlammalba by the hand.

Again the Ered laughed his orange bursts. The corrected picture showed the Ered trudging steadily, with a Vlammalba darting back and forth in spirals about the line of his march, filling the air with its feathery presence. The message was plain, no walker ever led a Vlammalba by the hand.

But he evidently understood her meaning, for he again laid his hand on her wrist, touched Alice's case lightly, and slipped out through the window panel. Ila could see his small, lumpy shape go trudging away into the surrounding trees.

"For a very first attempt at contacting alien intelligence, that wasn't so bad," she said, trundling Alice back into position. "And our light seems to have frightened the livestock away. I'll leave the lamp beside the window, and maybe we . . . I mean I . . . can get some sleep. Good night, Alice, my friend. Let's hope the Vlammalba is as congenial as the Ered."

But sleep didn't come soon. Ila lay quiet in the foampack, listening to the alien night-sounds, the unfamiliar noise of the wind in strange leaves, the distant calls of creatures that walked in the darkness. And when she slept at last, she dreamed of winged beings soaring in skies punctuated with slim-toothed mountain peaks.

CHAPTER THREE

Vlin poised on her toes, gazing through the delicate arch of her window at the crystalline morning. In the dawn light, flushed to a pink glow, the peaks round about soared into the chill lavender of the sky. Some of her sisters were already spinning dizzily or dancing aerial daisy chains in the intoxicating freshness of the new day, but she let her wings droop and turned away, back into her chamber.

The Ered by the door looked at her questioningly, picturing her own shape, dazzlingly white-feathered, her skill only improved by her great age, among those greeting the dawn, but she smiled and said, "I have no zest for the morning dance, Ered. The taste of my life has gone, and only lava dust is in my mouth. Perhaps it is the project of the young ones that disturbs me. It is difficult for one so old as I to accept the changing of all our ways of living. Do you, perhaps, speak in pictures with those of your kind who dwell with the Vlammere? Are they also dissatisfied with the ancient ways?"

Again the pictures formed behind her eyes. Vlammere in a group, their winged shapes taller than her own, as was natural in males, the rose-shaped organ on their chests slightly larger and more cupped.

They seemed to be arguing among themselves, but as she looked more closely she saw that those who stood silent were all white-feathered, while those who spoke and gestured with vigor bore the dark bandings of youth upon their wings.

"Strange," she mused. "After so many, many thousands of years. Why should the young now want to live in one place? Our longfathers divided our race for a reason, in the lost years, and we should go warily before we overset their workings. But who am I, who have long since made my last mating flight and brought my hatchlings to maturity, to hold out my hand and say, 'Stop' to the evolving of our race?"

The Ered made no more pictures but sat by the door, his sad eyes following Vlin as she moved across the chamber to her worktable.

She perched lightly on the tall stool and looked at the calculations of the day before. Even mathematics had lost their old flavor. The orderly progressions did not soothe her, nor did the logic bring a smile as it always had.

"I have almost completed my task," she said to the Ered. "Every known sun of our galaxy is here in my chart, with its past and future motions and even its probable planets. But I take no satisfaction in it. Oh, Ered, I need something new!"

There was a burst of song at the door, trilling in heart-stopping cadenzas to a climax of pure joy.

"Enter," said Vlin, and her trill was in a minor key, holding no joy at all. She winced as the translucent stone that formed the door moved upward and Hla wafted under it.

If ever a Vlammalba could be said to bounce, it was Hla who most nearly achieved it. Her youth, her fine health, her bursting spirits filled the room. The organ on her feathery chest glowed delicately pearl-pink, the bands on her wings were a gray that was almost lavender. Her whole being sang with beauty and a bursting vigor.

"Vlin!" she trilled. "Are you not well? You were not in the morning dance!"

Vlin looked down at her tables of figures. "No," she said. "I may be going away, my daughter. I am not ill, but weary, I think, with too long living. The old joys and the new problems alike give me no interest, no joy, and what is a Vlammalba without joy? Our whole lives are music and mathematics and love of living. If any of these fail, we are hurt, indeed, and all have failed for me. I must go away from the high places for a time.

"I may take myself down to the forested lands and lie beside the brooks and walk beneath the trees. I may even visit the Vlammere—" here Hla gasped with shock—"oh yes, child, I can visit the Vlammere at any time, now that I am too old for mating. It is only the young who become intoxicated with one another to the detriment of work and learning. The old enjoy other things, but quietly. And with the unrest among you all, I truly believe that I would do well to greet Vleer, your father, and to talk with him concerning this projected changing of our lives."

Hla looked troubled. "I did not realize that our talk had come to your ears, my mother. We are not rebellious . . . not yet, . . . but we are not happy. Those of us who have yet to make our first mating flight are not so concerned as are those who have a hatchling, but all are wondering and thinking and making ready for a change, for change moves in the wind. Had you gone among the peaks this morning, you would have felt its breath all about you. And all the Ered . . . have you noticed? All the Ered are excited."

Vlin turned to the Ered who sat by the door. His chisel was moving over the stone with its usual fine accuracy, and forests and flowers followed in its path, but there was an air of tension and expectancy that hung about him in an almost visible veil.

"Ered, my friend," she said and fluttered to his side, laying her hand upon his shoulder, "what disturbs you?"

His answering pictures were incoherent, inchoate, filled with bursts of orange laughter and points of chill blue questioning. Beneath her hand, he trembled.

"He doesn't really know, I think," said Vlin. "One of his kind has encountered . . . something, I surmise, with which he is unfamiliar, and all the Ered feel, without understanding, his bewilderment. And that is strange, for the Ered are old, old, and have seen all that our planet has to offer many times over. What the Ered do not know about Vlahil is not there to know, for it was they who set the feet of our fathers upon the road of learning, though they made little culture of their own . . . I have been taught, at least, that this is true. I have often wondered if there is not more to our Ered than we have ever learned."

Hla bounced impatiently to the high arch of the roof and settled again to the floor on tiptoe. "How can you muse over the Ered when it is you who are not well? We should call the Physician from among the Vlammere. What a bother that it is their time to provide a Physician. It is so much more convenient when it is one of our own, here among us. But we must send for him at once."

"Hla, you have not heard me. I said that I am well. Only my spirit is weary and unhappy, and that no physic nor massage will cure. Embrace me, for I shall not wait to speak with our sister Vlammalba. I go at once to the lowlands, and it may be that I shall find something new to give me laughter and music again."

Hla drifted to her side and held out her hands. They laid their lightly downed cheeks together and their hands palm-to-palm, then they parted and Hla moved to the door, looking back. But her mother gestured emphatically, and the young Vlammalba swooped under the portal and took to the air.

Vlin turned to her table and covered over the sheets of her calculations. From her perchlike couch she removed the silken coverlet and twisted it expertly into a package, no larger than her hand, which she put into a small pouch together with a fire-maker and a fold of paperlike stuff and a marking stick.

"Keep my house well, Ered," she said. "Unless you will go with me?"

But the Ered projected the pale green of a regretful no, and Vlin stepped gently through the door and swept into the sky. Her first thought was to sweep down the reaches of the mountains at once, but as she curved her flight to miss the nesting aerie she slowed and stooped to a landing on its doorstep.

The portal opened to her trill, and she entered, feeling in her heart the first tingle of pleasure in many weeks.

"Greeting, Hlere," she called to the young Vlammalba who came to welcome her. "I am beginning a journey, but I felt that I must refresh my spirit among the very young before I go. Are all well?"

"Well, Lady Vlin, and of most unabated spirits. Go you in to the nestlings, and I will continue my tasks."

The first low door opened into a great chamber, much warmer than that comfortable to adult Vlammalba. Row after row of eggs lay there, each in its own cradlelike nest, with wrappings that varied according to the tastes of the producers of the eggs. Some were there making their daily visits to their potential offspring, stroking and singing to the pearly ovoids, for it was believed that the embryo could hear, long before it came to hatching-time.

Vlin smiled tenderly and went through the chamber to a larger door that led into a tremendous domed room, which was padded, walls, roof and floor, with downy stuff. The reason for this was readily apparent, as infant Vlammalba and Vlammere flew soon after birth, and the air was alive with flitting bundles of down that crashed into one another, the walls, and the padded roof, with great impartiality.

Vlin caught a flying shape that hurtled by and cradled it in her arms, looking down into the face of a startled Vlammere. His incipient tears turned to chuckles as she brought her wing forward and tickled his nose with her feather-tips.

"Will you, youngling, also wish to change our world?" she asked him, reaching up to release him into the freedom of the air. "Or will you go down to your brothers, in a year, and be content?"

Smiling, now, she retraced her steps and sprang from the stone, borne up as much by the happiness always given her by the young as by the strength of her pinions. And now she went down, circling in the cool downdrafts and spiraling lower and lower as she left the lofty peaks behind.

Below, she could see the fine green haze that was the forested land, the silver loops of the streams that watered them and the grasslands to the west, the grouping of isolated rock formations, seeming small from her lofty height but in reality towering escarpments, that formed the home of the Vlammere.

Her untiring wings bore her down and down, until she came to rest beside a small brook that hurried down the slope of the forest floor toward the river that flowed beside the Vlammere's home. She bent over the stream, laving her hands in its live coolness, splashing it over her face, feeling almost young in the watchful restfulness that was the forest.

CHAPTER FOUR

The sun rose, outlining the stiletto peaks to the east in rosy fires. The shapes of the mountains were flat silhouettes in purple parchment against that ardent glow, and Hliss gazed, enraptured, at those enchanted heights. There dwelled Hla, his sister-mate whom he had never seen. The juices of life stirred strongly within him, and he turned from his arched window and fluttered across the lofty chamber, agitation reflected in every feather.

The deep notes of the morning song echoed across the face of the escarpment that the Ered, long, long ago, had carved into lacework on its face and chambered halls within as a home for the Vlammere. He, too, was avoiding the morning rituals, leaving empty his place in the choir of winged shapes that moved in complex patterns above the river flowing at the foot of the rock. The sound of the solemnly joyful voices was rather thin on this morning, and Hliss suspected that others were also absent.

The Ered who sat by the door had brought a cup of broth and a small brown loaf for his first meal, and Hliss paused by the elaborate shelf where they sat, musing as he ate upon the carvings that the Ered had liberated from the stone of the mountain that was the wall. That artful design and delicate imagination could emerge from such lumpish beings as the Ered had always intrigued him and did so now, even in the midst of his personal turmoil.

"My friend Ered, how came your folk to serve mine, I wonder? You have no need of us that I have ever discerned, though we have much need of you. What strange circumstance brought our races together?"

There came into his mind a picture . . . a line of Ered facing a line of Vlammere and a line of Vlammalba, all three ranks of which extended away from him in diminishing size until the ends were lost in the reaches of perspective. Nevertheless, though its meaning was clear, he felt that there was an ambiguity, some obscured . . . deliberately? . . . factor that would explain that long association.

Finishing his meal, he dismissed the thought and moved past the Ered into the vaulted hallway that led deep into the many-chambered mountain. Lifting, he flew with some urgency toward his goal, and as he flew, his inner disturbance mounted, and the rosy organ on his chest blushed red. Hler, the young Vlammere who waited outside a tall door before him also bore the stigma of emotional stress, but they laid palm to palm in greeting, then entered the chamber to meet with their peers.

It was a deeply troubled group that awaited them. Hleeth, Hlen, Hlet, Hlor, Hlant, Hloor, all their hatchmates, as their names signified, were in the midst of a heated discussion, losing their poise enough to lift at unexpected moments, which gave the group an unsettled and erratic appearance. But they settled to the floor upon the entrance of Hliss and Hler, and the burble of talk quieted.

Hleeth greeted both, as Eldest-by-Days, and said, "We are agitated, my brothers, as are you. Though we talk and argue among ourselves, we have yet to present our problem to the Eldest. And as he is your own begetter, Hliss, we feel that you are that one to whom the task must fall. Will you undertake it, in our behalf?"

Hliss settled to his heels, an act which he did not often accomplish. His down-covered face could not grow pale, but his feathers quivered with agitation. The bluish-gray bands across his wings rippled as if a breeze had touched them, and his hands buried themselves in the down of his breast. Then he raised his eyes, and his incisive features settled into firm lines.

"I will do it, brothers, though it pains me to bring pain to my father, who has always dealt fairly and tenderly by us all. He, being Eldest, will have many thoughts that we are unable to appreciate, I have no doubt. But I will take our case to him, and I will argue as well as I am able for the merging of the two halves of our race into one again, as it must have been in the remote time-before-remembering."

The brothers gathered about him, touching, one after another, palm to palm, murmuring their thanks. Hleeth, coming last, said, "An end to our unrest may yet come, Hliss. Hasten to your father, that we may know soon."

And Hliss, bidding them good-bye, did hasten away to the outer door, launching himself into the bright sunlight of midmorning. As he whirled above the river, racing his shadow across the face of the escarpment, he rehearsed in his mind the arguments that he must present to Vleer.

The graceful lines of his father's balcony came too soon into view, and he landed cleanly upon it, calling greeting to Kli, who was Second-Eldest and the sharer of his father's aerie.

The basso notes of Kli's answer rolled out to meet him, and he entered the room that was his father's study. All about the walls were the intricate mechanisms of Vleer's invention. Devices to record the music of both the Vlammere and the Vlammalba sat beside spool after spool of threadlike recordings. One wall was webbed with fine-spun wiring, winking lights, humming speakers that suddenly muttered messages from other Vlammere who made their aeries in distant places. The transmission and recording of sound was the passion of Vleer's mind, and in this he had found an enthusiastic assistant in Kli.

For Kli was the lover of metals and their working. He had found others who delved into the deeps for ores, with the aid of the Ered, who did the labor that the feathered ones were unable to accomplish with their light bones and specialized muscles. He had designed smelters and invented mechanisms that drew out copper and silver into wire, that purified iron into steel (though iron was rare on the world of Vlahil, and the use of it was limited). The two old Vlammere had worked together in creating a system of communication that gave great joy to the older Vlammere upon the greater continent of the planet.

The younger of their kind, those still of mating age, were indifferent. The mating flights were the substance of their thoughts and their dreams. Only once a year did they consider themselves truly alive, and their elders held them to their studies and their work only with great difficulty in the long months between summer solstices.

So it was that Hliss paid little attention to the fascinating fruits of his father's labors, as he entered the chamber he had so seldom visited before. He fluttered his wings in a formal salutation to Kli and asked, "Is Vleer within? I have a thing to say to him."

The twinkle in Kli's eyes would have been obvious, had Hliss not been so absorbed in his errand. But the old Vlammere only said, "I shall call him. He has reached an age when the rising of the sun no longer rouses him with its soundless chords, and he sleeps long, these summer mornings. Await him here, youngling."

Hliss glowered at Kli's retreating back. His maturity was too new and tender to allow such levity, and the thought of his own youth was like grit in his craw. But he said nothing and fluttered over to the wall of communicators, watching the lights flicker and listening with an indifferent ear to the distant voices of his people as they conversed across the miles.

Then a thought came to him. At the mating flights of the last summer he had been a spectator, though still too young to participate. Another spectator of his own age had been a Vlammere from far over-mountain, Zlir by name, and the two had found much to talk about and many areas of agreement. The name of his aerie was Eliss, and there on the panel before him was a button with the exquisite scrolled symbols that spelled out "Eliss." Touching it, he found to his delight that a voice answered immediately.

"Llin is here, Caller-Through-the-Void. What do you require?"

"I wish to speak with Zlir, Wise One, if it is permitted," answered Hliss, then held his breath.

There was a long pause, then Llin said, "Young Zlir is here; you may proceed."

Pitching his voice low, Hliss said, "Do you remember me, Hliss of Rhoosh? We met at the mating flight and found much delight in one another."

There was a short pause, then Zlir's voice came. "True, I remember Hliss. But I did not think to hear your voice until midsummer again."

Hliss sighed. "There is change in the air, Zlir my friend. We here in the Aerie of Rhoosh are charged with strange thoughts that we need to share with others of our kind. Will you bring those of your hatchmates who seem ill-content with the old ways and meet with us in the evening of the fourth day hence?"

There was another, longer pause. Zlir's voice was cautious as he replied, "We are young, and that means discontent. Yet my hatchmates seem more so than most. We will come."

Then the connection was severed, and Hliss turned to the susurrus of his father's wings at the door.

He fluttered his wings deeply in obeisance, and Vleer said, "Well come, my child. What brings you to my chamber, and so early in the morning, when your mates still circle the heights, taking joy in the morning?"

Hliss stood for a moment, gathering his self-assurance. At last he said, "You know, Father, that all within Rhoosh love and revere you, and that I, being your son, do so more than any. But there is unrest among my peers, and even among those somewhat older than are we who have made mating flights. We feel that the long tradition of separation of male and female upon our world is a thing outmoded and useless. Our hearts cry out for the constant companionship of our mates and for the pleasure of attending the hatching of our young. We feel cheated.

"Among all the other beings and creatures of Vlahil, only we are so segregated, for even our avian cousins nest together and nurture their young in partnership. The Ered live together in their caverns, though none save they can know which of them is male and which female. All the beasts live so. We are afire with the need for change. The very air about us is charged with a different energy. We believe the time has come to discard the old ways and to change the ancient pattern."

Vleer listened quietly, his wings stirring gently in the breeze from the balcony. His snowy plumage did not rise in ridges, as it would have had he felt threatened by his son's words, but his face was set in lines of doubt.

When Hliss fell silent, Vleer took his hand and led him to the balcony door. "Look out over our world, my son. We possess it in peace, without enmity from any creature that shares it with us. All work in harmony for mutual benefit. Yet it is in my mind that this is not a natural state, that it was brought about in the far-past ages, either by our own people or by . . . others. We do not know what factor in our lives or our environment sustains this condition, though many generations of our people have studied the question. On the small continent upon the other side of our world there are none of our kind, nor of the Ered, and there beasts prey upon beasts, winged ones upon winged ones, and each upon the other. There is no order there, and no peace.

"There is a danger that any major change we bring about might upset the balance that makes Vlahil a place where there is peace for the making of music, of mathematics, of mechanisms, of philosophies and dreams. We have no way of knowing what the reason was, long ages ago, when our race was divided. What if that one circumstance is the thing that holds our world in check?

"It will require far more than my own consent, or even that of all the Elders of Rhoosh and of Rhooshal to make that change. All the Vlammalba and Vlammere of our world will be vitally concerned, and all must agree before this might be done. Have patience, and counsel your brothers to patience also. I will set the question before our race, but you must abide by the decision that is reached." Vleer curved his wing tip to touch Hliss upon the brow, and the younger bowed his head and turned from the balcony into the wind of flight.

But his young heart cried out within him, "Why do the old make complex so simple a thing as change?"

CHAPTER FIVE

Ila woke from a sleep that had refreshed her whole being and lay for a time looking through the window into the green and gold of the forest that lay behind her hut. The early sun streaked the foliage with shifting light, and the branches seemed alive with small creatures that climbed among the leaves, picking what might have been buds and popping them into their mouths.

From time to time a bird with smoke-gray wings and trailing tail feathers rose from one tree, pursuing some insect, perhaps, and settled into another. But its motions disturbed no one of the little creatures, nor did the antics of larger animals that Ila identified as her teddy bear with luminous ears, though the luminosity was quenched by the sunlight.

At last she rose and folded away her foampack. Touching Alice's button, she said, "You know, Alice, if the Instrumentality knew what a nice place they've sent me to, they'd take me back and send me someplace else, I'll bet. There are about ten sorts of creatures out there in one clump of trees, and not one is killing or eating another. And if the Ered comes back, we'll have someone to communicate

with, too. Not to mention his Vlammalba. What if
. . . but it's better not to set our hopes too high.
How are you this morning?"

Her question was only half-joking. Already, she
felt that Alice was a fellow human being who only
happened to live inside a black metal casing.

"I really need a dose of sunlight, dear," replied
Alice. "We used a lot of my stored energy yesterday,
and I need a recharge. I feel quite used-up."

"I should have thought!" exclaimed Ila, taking
Alice in her two hands and trundling her out into
the morning sun. Before touching the button again,
she asked, "Now is there anything else you need—
oil or anything?"

Alice chuckled. "No, all my parts are either sealed
or non-moving. Sunlight is all I need. Go and eat
your breakfast, then come out and we'll wait for the
Ered to come back. . . . I have a feeling he will."

So Ila hurried through her meal, cleaned her ugly
dwelling as much as needed, and went out to lie in
the grass beside her Companion. Again touching
the button, she asked, "Have you the Mozart piano
concerti? And are you recharged enough to play
them for me, one after another, all the way through,
if we have time?"

Instead of reply, Alice poured forth the mathematically perfect spirit of Mozart into the unsuspect-
ing air of Vlahil. And the chittering and scurrying of
the animals in the wood halted. Ears of all sizes and
colors twitched toward the hut. The mouse with
hands, which had examined her house in the night,

crept out into the open grass and lay gazing at Alice as if hypnotized. Only the bird took to the air, and it seemed to be dancing an aerial ballet, following the melodic line with its intoxicated motions.

Ila lay in the grass, totally entranced. Nothing in her whole experience had prepared her for such a reaction in lower forms of life. The kinship of enjoyment united her, for the moment, with all the beasts of the wood and with the joyful bird. The sun mounted the sky, thrusting its fingers among the branches of the wood, lighting the furred faces among the twigs, the row of Handmice (as Ila had christened them), the Earbears clinging in the crotches of the trees, vague shapes of the spidery creatures, which crouched in the shadows, rounded lumps that were the Spherepigs.

So enchanted was the time, so enthralled were all the listeners, that no one saw or stirred when the Ered trudged into the clearing, with Vlin, whom he had met in the forest, soaring above him. Both came to a halt, Vlin alighting soundlessly beside her escort. They stood listening to a music so new, so alien, so mathematically ecstatic that it almost stopped the breath in their breasts.

Through the many concerti of Mozart Alice played, as the sun mounted to noon and past, Ila watched with wondering eyes, the beasts listened, and the two incomers marveled. When at last the concert ended, there was a long time of silence, then the little creatures shook themselves and moved into the trees, the larger ones stretched their stiff

muscles and returned to the deeps of the wood, and
Ila sat up and saw the Ered and Vlin sitting on the
grass behind her, Vlin's wings trailing out behind
her like a feathery train.

She stood, awkwardly, and the two stood also. Ila
felt, somehow, that she was about to meet a being so
royal and wise that it existed on a different plane
from that which she had known all her life. She
suppressed an impulse to attempt a curtsy; she drew
in her elbows, which suddenly felt all a-gawk, and
tried to align her feet into a less ducklike position.

Vlin, watching, drew many inferences from Ila's
unease. Though this was a being whose species, sex
and mind were totally unknown to the Vlammalba,
Vlin had had long years of experience in dealing
with the young, and this creature, she knew unerringly, whatever else it might be, was young. Alice
she accurately assessed as a mechanism, much akin
to those her brother-mate Vleer had spent his life
creating.

The Ered had watched the meeting with his sad
green eyes, and now he moved forward, beckoning
to Vlin to approach Alice. He laid his hand on the
black case, and Vlin followed suit. Ila touched the
translator key, then laid her own hand beside the
lumpy one and the long, white hand covered with
finely cut feathers along the tracings of the bones.
Alice said, "Speak, Ila. Give me something to work
on."

At her words, Vlin started, but Ila said immediately, "I don't know who you are, or what position

you hold here, but I am honored to meet you. You are the most beautiful being I have ever seen in all my life." Then she gestured toward Alice, and the Vlammalba, sensing the purpose, trilled a long series of notes that wove delightful patterns in the air so lately tenanted by Mozart.

"No wonder you loved the music!" exclaimed Ila. "You sing your language . . . how lovely!"

Vlin's fine-cut lips were not designed for smiling, but the corners of her eyes crinkled in what could only be a sort of smile. Alice's expertise was so efficient that already she had gained enough common ground to convey a part of Ila's meaning to the alien. The Ered, ever attentive, broadcast an aura of pale-pink approval over the entire proceeding, then he gestured toward the shaded grass in the wood, and Ila, taking the hint, moved Alice so that all could sit on the cool green and touch the black case.

So the afternoon wore into evening, and many words and notes were spoken and sung into Alice's patient ear, and her intricate system digested all and at last began to sort out concepts, nouns, and verbs. By moonrise, Vlin and Ila were able to exchange greetings, and immediately Ila said, "I hunger, Lady Vlin. My house, food, you share?"

Vlin looked long at the harsh lines of the hut, but she suppressed her opinion and said, "Yes, Friend Ila. I hunger; I will share."

The Ered, sensing, it may be, the state of Ila's stores, disappeared into the wood for a time, returning with creamy fruit, tart stalks that looked somewhat like celery, and a root that gave off the homely smell of onion.

Ila, given the stimulus of company, resurrected her culinary imagination and, using generous amounts of onion, broiled tasty fritters compounded from the formerly bland goo of her basic ration. This, with the Ered's contributions, made a fine repast, and the three sat in amicable, though rather incoherent, talk until the night was old. At last, Ila unrolled her foampack and gestured toward it, but Vlin, with her odd smile, motioned to the wood, sketched a tree with graceful motions, and laid her head upon her hand, as in sleep. The Ered also offered his pale-green "no," and moved away into the wood.

As Vlin emerged from the doorway, Ila hurried after her and ventured to touch her wing. The Vlammalba turned, and Ila said wistfully, "Tomorrow? You will come?"

Vlin examined the girl's face closely in the moonlight, then she bent her wing forward and stroked her cheek with the wing feathers. "Yes," she said. "Tomorrow; I come."

When Ila returned to the hut, she spun on her toes for a dizzy moment, then touched Alice. "My dear Alice, we have found a friend . . . two friends, really . . . on Vlahil. The first day, actually. The Instrumentality seems awfully far away and unimportant, doesn't it?"

"I wonder," Alice mused, "how many of the exiles are rejoicing that the computers sent them off-

Earth? The System would be horribly shaken if many are in our condition. But Ila, dear child, remember that you will become lonely for your own kind. You are young and have no child and no prospect of ever having any. Don't fly too high, for coming down with a thump isn't pleasant."

Ila patted the shiny black case. "Nothing can be perfect, old dear. Let me enjoy what I can, and I'll promise not to whine when the doldrums hit. All right?"

Alice hummed, then clicked. "All right. Good night."

CHAPTER SIX

Vleer mused long, after his son had left him. Something he knew already of the unrest among the young, though the why of it was obscure to him, as to the others of after-mating years. Why in this time? For thousands of summers there had been no questioning of the ancient law . . . what element of disquiet rode the spring winds and unsettled the hearts of the young?

Kli interrupted his thought with a firm reminder that his morning food was waiting, and he looked up at the waiting Ered apologetically.

"Forgive me, Ered. I was discourteous." He reached for his broth bowl, expecting to find in his hands the lovely shape of porcelain from the Aerie of Hleesh that had held his fare for seasons beyond remembering. But the Ered held forth a rough bowl of stoneware, filled to the brim with appetizing broth, but unfamiliar and disturbing.

Vleer stared at the thing in his hands, then at the Ered. But that lumpy being gestured for him to drink, and the old Vlammere raised the bowl to his lips and downed the mixture before again looking to the Ered for explanation.

"What troubles you, Ered?" he asked. "Some-

thing there must be, for you have never behaved in
this way before now. What moves in the morning
wind to ruffle your mind and unsettle your heart?"

The Ered stood, then, and moved his strong and
flexible hand in an emphatic gesture toward the
south. He laid his head against the stone of the wall
and pantomimed sleep. His fingers came walking up
the wall to his forehead and tapped thereon, and
Vleer knew that a dream had come to him in the
night.

"Show me the dream, Ered. What could you see
in the night that would walk with you into the light
of the day?"

Vleer closed his eyes, opening his thought to the
picture the Ered would project. But as the first
forms moved into his mind he staggered, and Kli
caught him in his arms to brace him against the
visions that now moved through both their minds.

Against a night sky, they saw the shapes of
Earbears asleep in the treetops, swaying slightly as
the branches moved in the summer breezes. There
was other movement also, and the two Elders
watched in horror as a Spiderbeast crept softly
along a branch, dropped onto a sleeping Earbear,
and fastened its thornlike teeth in its throat.

Another picture dawned in their inner sight. A
small yellow bird flitted in the moonlight, catching
insects. As it flew, darting and swooping to pursue
its prey, a larger bird shape appeared against the
moon and stopped upon it, catching it from the air

in claws that pierced it, dripping dark drops through the moonlit air.

An Ered trudged past their inner eyes, the shadows of leaves dappling his dumpy shape as he moved down a forest path. He stopped suddenly, his head tilted as though he listened intently. He gave a jerk, his hands rising to his chest convulsively as he fell to the leaf- and moon-littered path. His hands fell, and they saw on his breast a round, reddish puncture, burned at the edges, in which black blood welled, overflowed, and sank back to rise no more.

Vleer gasped. "What would kill an Ered?"

Kli answered, his voice rumbling like an organ through the notes of his reply: "No creature of our continent . . . or of our world, I think. All who live in harmony in the lands we know depend upon the Ered for care in sickness, for food in time of famine, for comfort in affliction. No beast or being known to us would slay one."

Vleer turned again to the Ered. "Where? From what direction did these terrible dreams come? Well we know that what your people see has happened, or will happen in future. Where must we look for this sickness that comes upon our world?"

The Ered again gestured southward, emphatically. Then he turned toward the northeast and signed for them to close their eyes again. Into their minds came a picture of a rough hut in a clearing among the trees. Before it stood a short, thick shape, unfeathered, unwinged, that bent over a black case. In the trees and on the grass about gamboled dozens of small creatures, and into the minds of the watching Vlammere came the vibrant rose color that was the Ered's color symbol for music. The shape of a Vlammalba approached, and the picture dissolved.

The Ered looked closely at the two Vlammere and projected the lavender symbol for "aid." They stared at him, then at one another.

"There is a . . . strange being . . . in our lands to the northeast," sang Vleer. "There is unexplained death far to the south in the untended forests, where none dwell but the happy beasts and some few Ered who see to their needs. The creature to the north can aid us in our endeavors in the south, when we go forth to attend whatever is amiss there. And a Vlammalba has met with this being, so our people will not be unfamiliar to it. That is your message?" he asked the Ered, who washed him in a pink yes.

Kli moved to the communications wall, touching first one button, then another. Vleer came to stand beside him, and voices began to answer in a rising mutter.

"There are strange things abroad in the lands," said Vleer into his speaking-device. And he told listening ears in Eliss, in Hleesh, in Vlar and Klath and many other aeries the tale the Ered had told. "We must act together to find what is happening in the southern forests. In addition, we need to call a gathering of the aeries, before midsummer mating, for the purpose of finding the cause and the solution of the unrest that has arisen among the young in some of our aeries. For many seasons there has been no problem in all the lands of our people. Now there are two, both of great importance. Truly, we live in strange times, and the winds are charged with change."

The voice of Rlith, the Eldest of Hleesh, came through strongly. "Our own Ered are disturbed, but none of us lie so near the untended lands as do you, and our Ered received only blurred pictures and indecipherable emotions. And our own young are afire with the desire to unite our divided sexes. Truly, we must meet together, Vlammere and Vlammalba, old and young, but we must not meet in the Ancient Place, for there thoughts of the mating flights would distract the minds of the young to the detriment of our purposes. We must meet at the High Place of Union."

There was a clamor of surprised voices in a fugue of agreement and disagreement. After a time, Vleer was able to make himself heard to ask, "But who of all our folk knows where to find that most holy place? It is more a myth than a place to be reached by the wings of our kind. I am old, and I have studied long in the records of our people, but I have never found a map nor a reference to the way that leads there."

Rlith again boomed, "There is only one who can know, only one who could show us the way. Ask the Oldest Ered. She will remember, for hers is the lore of that oldest of races, the histories of both our peoples are engraved upon her memory, and all places of importance in any of the Scrolls are known to her. Rhoosh stands upon the River of Ered. Send to her, or go yourself, Vleer, and stand before her in her cavern beside the river. Ask the Oldest Ered. She will know."

"I will," said Vleer. "When I know the place, I will call the aeries again, that we may meet there swiftly and soon."

Kli closed down the humming board, quenching the hot debates that still raged among the aeries. Then he and Vleer stepped from the balcony and sailed against the wind, upriver toward the caves of the Ered.

The morning had warmed into noon, and the river flashed its reflections against their speeding white wings as they flew. Birds dipped and flitted about them, finding their nest-chinks in the wall of the escarpment that stood to the west of the river, and, even in their haste, the two Vlammere hailed them with cries of "Ho, little cousins! Peace be with you!" as they sped past.

Now the escarpment wall dwindled, gradually seeking the level of the land across the river. In the tumbled rocks that lay before them, the Vlammere saw dark clefts and tunnels and knew that they had reached the Ered caves. There was no adornment cut into the rock faces. To one unfamiliar with the place, it would seem a place tenanted by animals. But Vleer and Kli well knew that behind those rough entryways were apartments of lovely proportions, decorated with stone-carving that excelled even that which the Ered executed for their own folk. But, like the Ered themselves, their homes showed no outward beauty, leaving the discovery of inner riches to those with the wit and the will to find them.

CHAPTER SEVEN

The cavern of the Oldest Ered was not easy for an outsider to discover. Its entrance was narrow and rather tall, opening between two tremendous boulders that leaned as if weary, one against the other, at a height somewhat inconvenient for the tall Vlammere. But when they found the small symbol of the Oldest cut unobtrusively into the stone, they cramped their wings closely about them and struggled through the opening.

At the boxlike passage that served as anteroom, they paused and called out, "Oldest, we are come from Rhoosh to ask you one question. May we enter?"

Their minds were immediately bathed in pink, and they went forward, past a set of offset screens carved into intricate patterns of leaf and vine and bud, into a large, light apartment that seemed full of sun and air, even buried as it was beneath the rocky hill. Aside from its lacework walls, there was little adornment and less furniture. Upon a low stool sat an Ered, working at something in a frame beside her.

As they entered, the Oldest rose from her seat and motioned to them to sit upon cushions that lay scattered about the floor. They arranged their wings and their knees with such dignity as they could muster, noting all the while the lovely needlework in unobtrusive shades of gray and tan and sage-green that was worked into the fabric of all the cushions about them.

"Your skill with the needle has not been told of you in the halls of the Vlammere," said Vleer. "No less an artist are you who work in cloth than those of your people who shape the face of stone."

The old Ered sat again upon her stool, and to their intense astonishment they heard within their minds a wispy, whisperish voice uttering words, a thing not within any experience of their folk in dealing with the Ered. With wide eyes, they listened as she said into their spirits, "You are courteous, Eldest of the Vlammere. And I am aware of the nature of the question you must ask.

"For seasons beyond the memory of any living thing . . . even I . . . our peoples have been bound by a common need. You know what the Ered give to you, but have you never wondered what it is that you supply to us that we cannot make for ourselves?"

"Often I have wondered," Kli rumbled. "None has ever answered my queries. Tell me, Oldest, can you relieve the wondering of a hundred seasons?"

"Yes," she said. "You can make music. Our folk cannot, being without voice. But music is as vital to our lives as air and food, and this you supply to us in unending variety and living beauty. So we are bound in common cause. And in the south lies something that slays Ered . . . that causes the beasts to kill for food, though there is no need, for our people there maintain and regulate all according to the needs of the many beasts.

"There must be a meeting of all our folk, Ered as well as your own. And the words of Rlith of Hleesh are good. It must be at the High Place of Union. That road is within my memory, but it is buried deep, and I must seek it out. The ways of remembering things anciently hidden are long and complex, and you may find your wait is lengthy. But, if you wish, you may come with me and lend your spirits' strength to my own, that the task may be shortened."

"We will come," said Vleer. "Yet one more question I must ask, Oldest. How is it that you, of all your people, may send words, instead of pictures, into the minds of the Vla?"

She smiled, as much as an Ered could, her lumpy face wrinkling into yet more complicated folds and projections. "I am old, old, Vlammere. For most of my lifetime I have sought to shape my thoughts into the forms you know, for it has been my intuition that one day we might need to communicate more closely than is possible in pictures. The symbolism of the Ered thought can be transferred to your minds only in its most elemental forms, so that abstract concepts cannot be conveyed with clarity. The effort I have made is very great, the difficulties enormous, for our minds do not perceive and communicate in the way yours do. This is the first time there has been opportunity—or need—for this sort of mind-speech, and I am well pleased that you and I can merge our thoughts so well."

She rose again from her stool and gestured for them to follow as she moved toward the rear of her chamber. In the far recesses of that huge apartment there was a small opening hung with tapestries that were embroidered with scenes of a forest by moonlight. So real were the shadowy tree boles, so lifelike the interplay of moonbeam and leaf-shade that the Vlammere felt, when they parted the curtaining fabric to pass through, that they should be entering an actual night-bound wood. But beyond, there was a low tunnel . . . though its shape was so harmonious and its finishing so smooth that the word does little justice to the passage through which they now followed the Oldest Ered.

There was light, though for a time Vleer and Kli were uncertain as to its source, for there was neither lamp nor torch, and there was no glow in the stone as there was in the aeries of the Vla. The light grew dimmer as they went deeper into the rock, and they were able to see, at last, that it came from transparent panels set into the rock.

"Oldest!" called Vleer. "How comes the light so deep into the earth? We see no artificial source."

There was a brief burst of orange chuckles, then the inner voice said, "There are vents cut through to the surface. Our forefathers set into these reflectors to carry the light down into the deeps, so that all the

Ered, though safely underground, could live in sunlight and good air. The panels you see are lattices, through which air moves, also."

She did not slow her pace and, short as she was, the Vlammere were forced to hurry their long legs to keep pace. At the last curve of the tunnel, she paused. The stone that now faced them seemed solidly a part of the hill, but the little Ered laid her small, strong hand against a flower incised into the rock, pressing her fingers against the petals in a complex order. For a moment, there was no response, then the stone quivered in its place and began to tilt. So delicately was it counterbalanced that there was no sound as it rose into a slot that had seemed only shadow.

The old Ered beckoned to them, and they compressed their long limbs and sweeping wings as well as they could and slipped through the doorway that was revealed. Beyond it, the walls fell away to left and to right, the roof arched high, and they were silent as they moved into a chamber that dwarfed all others they had ever seen. The light was no longer that of day and sun but of twilight, growing dimmer as they made their way deeper into the chamber. At a point halfway across that huge expanse of floor, the Oldest halted and motioned to them to be silent.

In the gloom they could see a pillared canopy rising from floor to ceiling, its airy columns twisted and fluted with consummate grace. In its center there was a stone bench, laid thickly with embroidered cushions, and to this the Ered went, lying flat and motioning for them to set themselves at her head and her feet. As they went between the columns, they stopped as one to examine the formation of the stone.

"These were natural pillars, as are formed in caverns," exclaimed Kli. "The Ered have smoothed them, perhaps, but the gods themselves shaped and carved them."

"This is our place where we seek out the gods," said the dry voice of the Oldest, within them. "You will find no carving of ours within this chamber. We found it as you see it, or our long-ago fathers did, perfectly formed, direct from the hands of Those Who Made All. We have added the bench, which is unadorned, and the cushions, for I, who use it most, have bones that are old and tend to ache upon cold stone. We love to reproduce the world about us, cutting it into enduring stuff like mountains and escarpments, but we come here to learn restraint in our art."

Vleer and Kli were now at their posts, and the Oldest laid her stubby hands upon her chest and closed her eyes. Once more they heard her voice, saying, "Close your eyes, also, Vlammere. Think of me and of your quest. Pour your strength into my aged being, that the gods may find it sturdy enough to bear the weight of their thought. They made all the ways, and surely they will help me to rediscover that one way that is lost among the years in the recesses of my brain."

It seemed very long to the two Vlammere, who

stood with patience, waiting. But suddenly they felt within their bones and veins a drawing away, as though something were pulling the strength from their sinews. They heard a gasp from the Oldest, and both realized how truly she had needed their bolstering of her energies. They held hard to their purpose, bringing from deep within all their reserves of will.

Yet, at last, they sank to their knees, Vleer first, for he was far older than Kli. As they knelt there, clinging to the stone bench, they saw behind their eyes bright shapes, slim star-shot forms that they recognized as the thoughts of the gods. Then they bowed their heads against their hands and wept that they had been given such a rare gift.

The voice of the Oldest Ered reached them in the midst of their despairing joy. "All weep who first see the working of the gods in their own spirits. But now we must take counsel, for I have been given the key to my own mind, and I now can show to you the way to the High Place of Union."

CHAPTER EIGHT

Vlin did not pause in the forest to seek out a tree for sleeping. After her afternoon with the alien creature, she was strangely troubled, though she felt no threat from either that being or her mechanism. But Vlin felt the need to communicate with Vleer as she had not felt so strongly in many years.

Though the moon would not rise for hours, she winged surely through the darkness, feeling with the inner sense of the Vla any troubling of the flow of air that indicated the presence of bird or treetop in her path. As she drew near to the escarpment, she felt it loom before her long before the glimmer of the river marked its place.

She had never seen Vleer's own apartments in that great warren, as he had never seen hers in the mountaintop. Their home, for the few months after each mating flight, had been a bower of flowering vines in one of the great trees in the old forest that bounded the Ancient Place. Now she approached the arched entryway, halfway up the face of the cliff, that led into the central halls.

There was a speaking device set into a niche in the wall, and she sang into it the notes that were hers and Vleer's alone. It was late, and she knew that

Vleer must be sleeping, as she would have been, husbanding his strength against the new day. But she felt compulsion, past any in her experience, and she sang again into the device.

A sleepy note in a bass voice answered, after a time, and she recognized with joy the voice of Kli.

"Forgive me, Kli, for disturbing your rest, but I must speak with Vleer. I am compelled by something I do not understand to come here, though it is late, and to tell him of a strange being in the forest."

"Wait for me, Vlin," sang the now wide-awake Kli. "I will come and guide you to our balcony. This day also brought to us an unusual adventure, and it may be that the two are parts of the same unease that haunts our roosts."

Vleer, beset by the problems of the past day, was not sleeping, and soon the three were deep in discussion of the strange events. The Ered who tended Vleer and Kli, wakened by whatever sense informed his kind of events of importance, came padding into the chamber soon after Vlin's arrival, and he brought a picture from the south.

The Vla closed their eyes, that they might perceive the image more clearly. From the mind of the Ered they drew a sense of night . . . then the picture cleared and they saw about them the tangle of the southern forest lands. The viewpoint moved, as though the Ered sending the message were turning slowly in his tracks. A gap in the trees came into view, and the Ered approached it. It disclosed a clearing upon a hillside that slanted downward from that point. In the clearing lay a . . . thing . . . unlike any they had seen before. It would have been invisible, for the night was dark and the moon not yet above the horizon, but in the space before it there was a dazzle of white light that washed the metallic bulk in hard-edged reflections and inky shadow.

Into the glare walked a stocky creature that brought a note of surprise from Vlin.

"This is like the being in the forest!" she hummed softly. "Not exactly like, perhaps, but of the same kind, I am sure."

The Ered in the south was moving toward the light, sending before him the quieting pattern his kind used in calming beasts and birds that became frightened. The figure before the shape straightened and peered into the darkness toward the Ered. It turned toward the metal bulk and an opening appeared, into which it crawled. After a time, as the Ered had almost reached the source of the light, the figure reappeared, followed by another, larger being, both holding what seemed to be short, wide-ended staffs.

The Ered now stood before the creatures, looking up at them from its lesser height. The watchers in the north could see, superimposed upon that which his eyes saw, the pictures he was trying to impart to the alien beings before it.

There was the forest, laid schematically across his mind, and moving upon that intricate map were the shapes of many creatures. At intervals a glow

marked the position of Ered among the other living
things, and the paths of the Ered guided those of the
others: the impression of care, of tending, of nurtur-
ing was plain. Then there was a strong yellow light
that washed over everything, the query of the Ered
. . . "Who are you? And how did you come to be in
our lands?"

The figures blinked. The smaller opened its
mouth, but sound was not transmitted by the Ered
abilities, and the watchers had no time to wonder
what it said, for the large creature pointed the staff
down at the Ered, and the picture dissolved into a
flash of scarlet, then blackness.

The Vla sat for a long moment in stunned silence,
then Vlin opened her eyes and cried out, the notes
wild and unmelodic, "Look to the Ered!"

That small being had fallen upon its side, curled
into a ball of agony. The Vla found water and damp-
ened its face, then carried it to Kli's apartment,
which boasted a large, soft matting in the corner
before his worktable. They laid the Ered carefully
down and huddled about him, wondering what
should be done. Never had any of them seen an
Ered in distress or in need. The fact that they didn't
even possess a couch fit for a creature that laid itself
down at night added to their discomfort.

Vleer touched the Ered on the forehead and
closed his eyes. "He is deep in blackness, but it is the
dark of sleep now," he said. "If this terrible picture
has reached many of his kind, there must be great
distress in the Ered caves. We must rouse our folk,

Kli, and go to their aid. For many lives of the Vla their kind have tended us with care and kindness, and we can do no less for them."

Kli nodded, his snowy plumage shining in the light from the glow-stones. He rose and went to the corridor that led into the depths of Rhoosh. In a moment an urgent chiming filled the great dwelling with vibration, and soon the air without and the corridors within were filled with the whisper of many wings.

Kli dispatched messengers to the Ered, then he organized others into groups to go to the aid of groups of Ered who lived southward, upriver from Rhoosh. And Hliss he sent directly to the Oldest Ered to inquire what might best be done for her people.

While the bustle was proceeding to order itself into purposeful patterns, Vleer and Vlin stood in a corner, out of the way, twittering softly to one another. And when Kli had completed his work, he returned to find them laying hand to hand, cheek to cheek in farewell.

"I must go back into the forest," said Vlin, "and bring back the being there. She can see through the mind of the Ered that found her, and she also has a device that is . . . or perhaps was . . . a being itself, and it is able to make meanings clear from mind to mind. We need them both, for she may understand the motivations of those creatures in the south, and her device will help us to understand her."

She stepped to the balcony and swooped away into the night, which was now dimly lighted by the rising moon. The air that flowed about her seemed charged with strange energies, and the winds through her wings sang of new times, new beings, new ways of thought and action.

The forest sped beneath her, and she began to tune her mind to the Ered pattern that should have been laid like a guardian across the wooded lands. But there was no feel of Ered in all the space about her, and she began to feel an apprehension that grew deeper as she drew nearer the part of the forest where the alien being had her dwelling.

Alighting at the door, Vlin sang a soft query into the night. Again she sent the notes into the air, and at last she heard the unmelodic voice of the being she sought. The door slid open, and Ila beckoned to her to enter.

Vlin went directly to Alice and stood with her hand on the case, gesturing to Ila to do the same.

Ila moved swiftly to her side, touched the button, and asked, "What is wrong, Lady Vlin? I feel you are troubled."

Vlin did not answer at once but took the girl's face between her hands and gazed deeply into her eyes, as if to search out the very bedrock of her being.

CHAPTER NINE

Ila had taken a long while to clear away the traces of the meal she had shared with her two alien guests. Somehow, that sharing had made the fact of her aloneness come home to her, now that the sun was down and night again had wrapped her hut in darkness.

When nothing remained to be done, she drew Alice over to the window and spread her foampack beside her, then touched the button.

"You were right, dear. I'm coming down off my cloud, and the bump is pretty hard," she said, as she laid her cheek against the shiny black case and stared at the window, which mirrored the pair of them against the blackness outside. "Can you give me a bit of poetry to liven things up?"

"How about 'The Hunting of the Snark'?" asked Alice. "You really don't need anything that takes itself seriously right now." And, without waiting for an answer, she began to recite in a rolling basso, complete with British accent, Lewis Carroll's inspired whimsy.

By the time the luckless Baker had met the Boojum and "softly and silently vanished away," Ila had recovered her natural optimism, to a degree.

"Honestly, Alice," she said, "you are wasted here with me. Why did they never think of making Companions like you to be entertainers?"

"Ha!" snorted Alice. "The Instrumentality finds no need for entertainment. Why do you think the theater disappeared? It couldn't be used strictly for propaganda without suffocation, so it died in a miasma of hot air. The holovee-casts are just a lot of painful garbage that the psycho-computers decree will twist the public's thinking toward whatever nitwittery the Unholy I is up to at any given moment. They did their dead-level best to get rid of all the books . . . but I told you about that, didn't I?

"Actually, when your father acquired me, I was scheduled to be scrapped. They couldn't bear the fact that so much of me came through that they couldn't use me just as a mechanism. I'd argue with them. They couldn't program lies into me, for I'd reject them. You've never seen anything until you've seen a Programmer who has been told he is a liar by the computer he tried to program." Alice giggled and her toplight flickered on and off in an intoxicated manner.

Ila lay back on her foampack and whooped. By the time she had laughed herself out, she was relaxed and sleepy and the world, wherever it was, seemed a much more cheerful place. She reached up and touched Alice's button, as she whispered, "Good night, old dear. Pup really knew what he was doing when he salvaged you." Then sleep rushed over her in a dark tide.

Strange fancies were walking through her dreaming mind when a melodious twittering broke into her consciousness, bringing her slowly awake. For a moment she lay, disoriented, until the anemic moon shining through the window recalled her to her situation. Then she recognized the song at the door as Vlin's, and she hurried up to greet her, lighting the lamp as she passed.

As Vlin looked deep into her eyes, Ila felt herself filled, like a jar, with the depth of the Vlammalba's perception; but there was no animosity, no desire to hurt, in that penetrating gaze. Instead, there was urgent need, and Ila stood steadily in its imperative survey.

Slowly, Vlin relaxed, her eye corners wrinkling in her strange smile. She turned to Alice, touched the button, and said to Ila, "The Ered . . . no feel of him here. Forests all feel of Ered caring. Ered all hurt by picture from the south. One dead there, all here saw and felt. Help me find the Ered."

Ila stared at the tall white shape. "You mean one of the forest creatures killed an Ered? Oh, I can't believe that! All the creatures I've seen are so gentle."

Vlin took her hand. "Not by forest creatures, Ila. By creatures like you. Two. There is a thing of metal, a white light, two beings shaped like you. One bears a strange staff, and that killed the Ered. When we find and help the Ered here, will you come with me to Rhoosh? We need your help."

"My . . . kind?" Ila stood, stunned. "There was

a scout ship, the computer said, lost in this sector. But why would they kill an Ered? I will come, Vlin. Now."

It was not possible to hurry through the wood with Alice in tow, and the Companion was a bit bulky for carrying easily. While Vlin circled above, scanning the wood for the Ered, Ila struggled along the uneven and root-ribbed paths below. And when Vlin gave a shrill call signaling success, the girl set Alice on the path with an apologetic pat and hurried in the direction of Vlin's voice.

The Vlammalba had found the Ered crumpled in a tiny clear spot, and the moonlight showed him in the same curled posture of agony that the Ered at Rhoosh had assumed. Ila knelt beside the small figure and felt for a pulse. Perhaps the Ered's vital forces were circulated otherwise, for she could find no pulse, no heartbeat, but the little being was alive. The indescribable tensions and electrical aura of life still clung to his body.

"Shock, I think," whispered Ila, straightening the lumpy figure on the grass. "I'd know what to do, if he were human, but he is so different. . . ."

Vlin bent above the Ered, then lifted him easily. "I will take him swiftly to Rhoosh, where my brother-mate waits. Then I will come for you. Wait." And she drove strongly with her wings and was aloft and out of sight.

Ila sat in the moonlight feeling almost disembodied, so strange and abrupt had been the last hours' happenings. About her in the forest were scurryings and scrabblings, sleepy calls and sharp chirps. She could see the glowworm aura of an Earbear high in a neighboring tree. As she watched, a hint of motion caught her eye at the edge of the moonlit patch. A Handmouse sat there on its small haunches, its hands folded neatly in its lap. The dim light sparked in its eyes as it tilted its head to look up at her. It seemed to be waiting for something, and suddenly Ila realized what it was. The Handmouse was waiting for music.

"I'm sorry," she said softly. "Alice is the one with the music, and she's over there on the path. I'm glad of your company, but I can't sing a bit."

The moon moved down the sky. Ila's head drooped, her eyes closed, and she slept, as the tiny beast watched and the wood breathed and moved about her.

It was not long before Vlin returned, so swiftly could she travel when necessity drove. Her light touchdown in the glade caused the Handmouse to chitter excitedly, and Ila woke to find the tall Vlammalba bending above her.

"We will find your mechanism and then we must hurry to Rhoosh. My brother-mate, Vleer, has found that most of the Ered are terribly unwell, after their shock of last night," Vlin trilled, and Ila looked up at her in astonishment.

"How is it that I understand you so well?" she asked. "I can follow your language easily, but I could not, before."

"You have slept in the wood, unshielded by walls.

The Ered have set the imprint of their minds on all the things of this continent, and understanding is the most precious of the benefits this conveys. But we will need your mechanism, also, to make things very plain between us.

"She was a person, once . . . she still is, in a way," Ila said. "I feel that she is one of my own people who just happens to live inside a black box."

Vlin knitted her downy brows. "Strange. The Ered will be interested to know of this. The mechanisms we make, upon their advice, are only devices for specific tasks. They have no character of their own. But we must hurry, now. Come, Ila, and I will show you the way to the path."

With the feathered guide fluttering above her, Ila found no difficulty in locating the path where she had left Alice, and she greeted the Companion with pleasure, touching the button that activated its cells.

"Alice, I can understand the Vlammalba," she said. "Vlin says that is because I slept in the wood without shelter and absorbed some sort of aura that the Ered put there." As she spoke, she was moving the Companion as swiftly as she could over the uneven path.

Alice's toplight blinked interestedly, but she said nothing as they hurried through the wood. But when they reached a broad meadow that extended, like a small sea, beyond the edge of vision, she said, "Ila, you simply cannot make any speed while moving me. Why don't you go with Vlin and send someone back after me?"

Ila had opened her mouth to reply when she saw
two silver-gray shapes arrowing over the meadow
toward her. Vlin trilled a shrill cry, which was answered in baritone carolings, and the two oncomers
redoubled their speed.

When they alighted, she saw that they were taller
and larger than Vlin. Their plumage was white,
banded with pale gray, and the rosy organs on their
chests were a brighter color and had a subtly different shape. Their voices and bearing marked them as
unmistakably male beings, though Ila could detect
in their manner an indefinable awkwardness that
revealed them as much younger than Vlin.

"These are Vlammere, Ila," said the old Vlammalba. "This is my son Hliss and his hatchmate
Hler. They have come in haste to bear you and . . .
Alice . . . to the aerie, though they have worked all
night among the Ered. Now we will go swiftly."

The young Vlammere were ill at ease in the presence of an alien. The fact that the alien was female
did not impinge on their minds until Hliss lifted Ila,
at which point he was confusedly aware of the fact
that she, whatever she was, was *not* male.

Ila felt his unease and kept up a running chatter
about the beasts and birds she had seen in the wood,
asking the names of the different kinds. So the
young Hliss was diverted from his embarrassment,
and the journey was made quickly.

When Ila looked ahead and saw the shining escarpment of Rhoosh rising in the morning river-
mists, she felt for a moment that she had been trans-

ported into a fairy tale or a myth. But the urgency
that infused the speeding form of Vlin, who flew
ahead of the burdened males, brought her to reality
again, and when her foot touched the stone of
Vleer's balcony, she was ready to cast her somewhat
doubtful might into the struggle that the feathered
people faced.

CHAPTER TEN

The Oldest Ered lay on her downy sleep-spot, her eyes closed, face lined in more-than-ordinary complexity. Though the Vlammere who stood nearby, waiting to attend any need she might have, did not know it, she had been conscious for many hours.

The totality of history that lay, three-dimensional and colorful, in her conscious and unconscious memory held many painful episodes, and the shadow of the pain felt by her remote ancestors was communicated also to her. But that was dim and far away, filtered through many lives and many minds. The pain that lived in her now was no long-preserved record but an immediate and searing thing.

Long as her life had been, full of the subtle work and planning of her people, she had never before felt the shock of panic fear emanating from living creatures. She had never experienced the unprepared-for, unrejoiced death of one of her kind. And now she understood the motivations of her long-ago people, when they took up the task of making a peaceful paradise of their part of Vlahil. No empath with the sensitivity of the Ered could exist for long in a world of fear without going into the chaos of madness or else foreclosing that empathic ability which was the root of communication for them.

So now she lay, resting her spirit from the terrible trauma it had known, letting her mind hover in the realms of almost-sleep, consciously knitting together the torn pieces of her serenity. For upon her, she knew, rested the well-being of all the Ered on Vlahil. And upon that well-being depended the peaceful survival of every sentient creature on the continent.

At last, she stirred herself upon the cushioned pile, and young Hlet, who had watched over her all night and far into the day, hurried forward. "Do you have need, Oldest?" he asked, and she nodded feebly.

Into his mind she projected the stylized images that represented Vleer and Kli, together with the chill blue-gray of urgency. The young Vlammere nodded in his turn, and hurried from the chamber.

Then she relaxed, deeply, deeply, and sent her remaining strength into her far-seeing ability. Over the forest and the low hills to the south, up into the foothills of the mountains, over the mountains, traced with the headwaters of the River Ered, down into the grasslands, and yet southward into the thick and jungled forests she fled. Always her thought probed the lands beneath, seeking for Ered.

But the Ered of the south were few and scattered, and she knew that they, being so near to the emotional catastrophe of the night, would have suffered devastating shock. So she went on, homing unerringly upon the spot where her fellow Ered had died. The forest below her speeding thought was quiet. The life that she should have felt in its restless multitude was subdued to a level beneath her perception.

The Oldest wondered, was it the death of the Ered, or was it even more the combined mental anguish of his fellows that had stricken the wild things to such quietude? In a world wrapped in thought-fields and tamed by mind, a mental whirlwind such as that must only be surpassed in destruction by an actual one. Perhaps all the birds and the beasts lay also in such a daze as did those Ered about her physical body overmountain.

Then she forgot the beasts, for her thought now felt a new aura, a new mental field. It was strong . . . unnecessarily strong for any purpose her people knew. And it had an undisciplined and primitive quality that she had no way of assessing, for those were attributes long ago eliminated from Vlahil. She had no doubt that the strange beings were its source, and she followed without hesitation where her instinct led her.

In that spot that every Ered within range had seen by white light lay the thing of metal. A device for travel, the Oldest surmised, far larger than any metallic thing ever made on metal-scarce Vlahil. The beings were not visible, but she rested patiently above, waiting.

While she waited, she felt, at long remove, the arrival of Vleer and Kli in her chamber, and with a vestigial sense she felt them approach and scan her untenanted body. With satisfaction, she felt them reach a conclusion as to her need, and when their hands grasped hers she felt a surge of strength and power that almost left her dizzy, disembodied though she was. She tuned her mind to theirs, that they might also see, and, all together, they continued to wait.

Had this Ered sense included hearing, they would have heard the aliens approach, long before they came into view, but the laden figures toiled into sight at last. They had killed beasts. The Oldest was wrapped in a thin mantle the color of anger, which no Vla had ever been able to describe, and her two helpers felt the backwash of her rage.

A Handmouse lay limply where they had dropped him, his little hands lax and his eyes open and no longer interested in all the world. Beside him was a Spherepig, his pale color already deepening with corruption. But the two who had slain them were not concerned. They built a fire, slashing away green growth and flowering vines from the spot they chose, and proceeded to skin and dismember their prey.

Now the onlookers could examine them closely. Vleer and Kli, having met with Ila, conveyed to the Oldest her image, and the three compared it with those below. Without doubt, they were the same species, though Ila was thinner and darker and her aura carried no fear. The color she projected to Ered was a lively pink, which, in its gradations in the Ered vocabulary, ranged from approval to sheer joy.

But these creatures carried in them a sickly green, like rotting fungus, and the Oldest knew them to be diseased and dangerous past her previous guess. Sorrowfully, she moved from them, returning to her flesh, and Vleer and Kli welcomed her with joy.

The old Ered lay still for a time recovering her strength and putting her wits in order. Vleer and Kli stood beside her, still holding her hands and pouring their energy into her, until she was sufficiently recovered to free her hands and motion to them to sit.

"Madness walks in the southern lands," her strange, whispery voice said inside their minds. "The one you showed to me . . . I must see her, feel her heart with mine. She is like, to the eye, but so unlike otherwise." She closed her eyes, and they could see the labored breath struggling in her throat.

The two Vlammere looked, eye into eye, and the same dire thought was in each of them. If the Oldest Ered should die, how might they find ways to deal with the problems that seemed to be inundating their peaceful existence? In her small, dumpy body, behind her wrinkled eyelids lay the store of all knowledge accumulated over the ages and the wisdom to use it well. Her successor had not yet completed training. There was no other among the Ered who could take her place at this moment.

Then Vleer, for the first time in his long life of deep thought and technical endeavor, felt the inner tickle of inspiration. Straight from the gods, he felt certain, came a thought so new and daring that he could not move for a moment as he considered it. Then he turned to Kli.

"My friend, last night, for the first time in our history, we were able to aid the Ered. Now I have been given another strange notion. We, you and I, will go into the inner being of the Oldest. We will, with the power of our minds, heal her as her kind have healed us for so long. We know, every one of us, the way of it, for we have experienced it so many times. Join with me, Kli, and we will make her well and strong, and then we may say that we have, in some little way, begun to pay our long debt to the Ered."

The Oldest felt their intent, knew their thought, but so weak had she become that she had no will in the matter. Yet something whispered to her that the gods had work, still, for her to do, and she lay in the cradle of their concern, bathed in the warmth of the thought of Vleer and Kli. And she felt the sliding senses firm to rationality, the laboring body ease. She knew in her bones a vigor that had been lost to her for long.

Then she opened her eyes and said, "You have done well, Vlammere. We had not known that you had learned our arts so carefully, or that you were capable of turning them to our help. Come what may, both our peoples will be the richer for the things we are learning now.

"But we must stir ourselves. There are dangers walking upon Vlahil that have not been here before, and old perils are stirring themselves and rising from their hiding places. We must meet with all who can arrive at the High Place of Union, to warn those whose homes are far from the troubled south of the madness that now dwells there. And we must take the unrest of the young and gaze upon it, to find its causes. It may be that the infection from the southern lands is at the root of that also."

CHAPTER ELEVEN

Ila perched on a spidery stool, her feet far above the mosaic patternings of the floor. Her eyes followed the flickering lights of Vleer's communications wall, and her ears frantically tried to sort out familiar words from the criss-cross babble of Vla that muttered from the speakers. She laid her hand on Alice, who was conveniently placed upon a shelf beside her.

"No evidence of intelligent life, says the remote scanner," she murmured, and Alice's toplight flickered in agreement.

"Typical Instrumentality incompetence," Alice said crisply. "The Roman Empire could have existed here, and if its buildings had been underground, and it hadn't needed roads, the Unholy I would have missed it clean as a whistle."

Ila turned to the Oldest Ered, who sat on another stool, her feet even farther from the floor than Ila's. Their eyes met and both smiled, though an Ered smile was a thing that required some getting used to. "Eldest," she said in careful Vla, "we feel neither love nor loyalty for the world that sent us here, even though it is the home of our race. Our world has been ruined by the self-interest of many groups of people over many thousands of years. Unlike Vlahil."

The Oldest's whispery voice rustled slowly in the girl's mind, and she knew the old Ered was slowing her projection in order that she might understand accurately.

"You had no Ered. You were infants turned, without teachers, into a world of wonders and dangers. It is a credit to your intelligence that you survived to go out into the freedom of space. The fact that your kind could combine metal with Man and produce Alice speaks well for them. I have learned more from her, mind to mind, than I could have struggled with language to learn from you in two lifetimes.

"Now I understand what the people in the south are and what sort of background they spring from. Through the understanding gained from you and Alice, I can . . . perhaps . . . find a way to reach their minds. But first, we must convene with the Vla at the High Place of Union, for we must have the thought of the gods before we move to constrain those who are not our own." The voice stilled, and Ila looked at the Oldest Ered in astonishment.

"We have been taught that belief in gods is a thing of ignorance and superstition. Though many of my people, by all reckoning, still believe, such belief is ridiculed and those who profess it openly are laughed at. Yet neither you nor the Vla seem open to such criticism. I am very much confused."

A trace of pink approval and a small burst of orange laughter burst from the Oldest. "Your confusion does you credit. But you will see, at the High Place of Union, the reality that we respect and obey, though we do not worship it. Perhaps your folk have no such place."

"They did once," said Alice softly. "It was called Mount Sinai."

Ila shifted uncomfortably on her high stool. "What was taught us on Sinai," she said, sighing, "might have saved us a lot of grief if it had been a lesson we had consented to learn. But it was mainly —you *know*, Alice—simple common sense. The rarest commodity on Earth."

Vlin turned from the communicators and wafted toward the strangely assorted three. "We will meet tomorrow . . . all the aeries, all the Ered the Vla can carry . . . at the High Place of Union. Hliss has seen that matting has been laid for you to lie upon, for our sleeping arrangements would not suit you at all. You both need to sleep now, for we will rise early and fly with first light. You, Eldest, are our guide, and you must be fresh. And you, Ila, as the sole representative of your race before the gods of Vlahil, will need to be alert. Go now, and rest."

Ila found to her surprise that Hliss also had made a spot for Alice at the edge of her pallet. But in the strangeness of the Aerie of Rhoosh the steady glimmer of her toplight was comforting, and she did not reach out and turn the Companion off. To her surprise, as she drifted into sleep, she felt the stubby hand of the Ered beside her touch her shoulder in an awkward pat and heard the dry voice say into her mind, "Sleep well, child."

Oddly enough, she did. No emanation of unease disturbed her, and she slept as she would have in her own father's home, wrapped about in concern and tender care. When the light hand of Vlin touched her shoulder to waken her, she rose refreshed and ready for the strange experiences this new day must bring.

Even in the bustle of a hurried meal, Ila found time to wonder at the lacelike stonework and the intricate needlecraft that decorated the aerie. The shelf on which her bowl and loaf sat was satiny-smooth on the top, but it rested upon a flange of pierced stone, representing a procession of beasts in a wood. Looking more closely yet, she found that the whole of the thing was a part of the wall that, in turn, was a bit of the cliff in which Rhoosh was set.

As she sat waiting to be taken up and carried away into the mysterious upper places of Vlahil, she talked quietly into Alice's patient records, describing the Vla, the Ered, the aerie, and her reactions to her exile so far. The most difficult thing to describe, she found, was the odor—or rather, were the odors —of Vlahil. The wood, though it had a green scent that reminded her dimly of Earth forests, had tangs and traces of unique plants and exotic animals. The Vla carried with them a faint smell of feathers that mingled pleasantly with the clean fragrance of the chill altitudes where they spent much of their time.

Rhoosh smelled of stone and spring water and

polished metals. Ila wondered what Rhooshal smelled like and determined that she would ask Vlin, should the opportunity ever arise, to take her to the aerie of the Vlammalba so that she might gather it, too, into the record of her senses.

As she sat, brow wrinkled, trying to put into words the small and acute personality that emanated from the Handmouse, Vlin again touched her shoulder and said, "The time has come to go. To begin with, Hler will bear you with him, Hliss will carry the Oldest Ered, and Kli will take Alice, that he and Vleer may communicate with her as they fly. The way is high—we must go over the mountains where Rooshal hangs—and the air is thin. We are not troubled by such things, as we are made for the high places, but should you be uncomfortable, wave to me and I will give you the air bottle I carry to aid the Ered."

Ila nodded, then found herself scooped up and borne away, out through the vaulted doors and into the heights above the escarpment. The sky about was dotted with flying figures, most of them carrying small shapes that were the Ered. Only the old, like Vlin and Vleer, were burdenless, and Ila saw at once that those unhampered figures were all snowy white, while the others had wings that were banded with all shades of gray.

The air was chilly, for the sun was just showing its disc above the distant mountains, but the rush of wind in her face was exhilarating, and Hler's feathery body against her side and back was warm and

pulsing with life. A peep over his arm showed the
land far below them, greened with sweeps of forest
and traced with silvery rivers, with great washes of
early morning shadow stretching away to westward.
Ila sighed with delight and gave herself over to enjoyment.

Those distant mountains drew nearer at an amaz-
ing rate, and the girl wished that she could ask Alice
her estimate of their rate, but Alice was thirty yards
away in Kli's arms, her toplight flashing vigorously
as she, evidently, carried on a spirited discussion
with him, Vlin and Vleer.

The sun was now above the sharp-toothed high-
lands, and the fairy-tale outlines of the turrets of
Rhooshal were becoming visible. Limned in plum
and blue against the brightness of the eastern sky,
their carven shapes displayed both the strength of
the original peaks from which they were cut and the
artistry of the Ered, who had sculpted them from the
stone of that high and windy place. The fretted balconies were sketched against the sky in lines of impossible fineness, and the low-relief carvings in the
faces of the aerie were highlighted in gold, their
depths still blue with the remnants of the night.

Music met the flying Vla as they moved over
Rhooshal, hundreds of finely tuned voices blending
in intricate harmonies, as the inhabitants of
Rhooshal winged upward to meet their Vlammere.
Ila felt the heart of Hler speed its rate as those
smaller, lighter shapes spiraled upward, riding the
currents of the air.

For a moment the upward drift of the Vlammalba mingled with the eastward line of Vlammere, but there was no confusion, no near collision. As if that joining had been choreographed by a master, the groups melded without wasting a moment, and all went eastward together as the sun continued its climb.

Now the air warmed, even at this altitude, and Ila slipped into a doze, waking now and again to look below. But only mountains lay there, growing, seemingly, steeper and higher with every league eastward. The air, too, was growing thinner, and at last the girl moved her hand, and Vlin dipped a wing in a soaring turn and came near, reaching to place a glazed vessel in the earthling's outstretched hand.

The bottle was spherical, and in the top there was a ceramic bud, flanked by two tiny leaves. Ila twisted, but nothing happened. Then she pressed gently on the bud, and a faint hissing told her that oxygen was escaping. She held it quickly to her nose and breathed in the reviving freshness.

After a bit, she closed the bottle and settled back to test her breathing. She smiled and handed the bottle back to Vlin, who immediately swooped away and offered it to the Oldest Ered, who took it eagerly. As Vlin moved away, her place was taken by another, and Ila looked aside to see another Vlammalba (she had learned by now to distinguish between the smaller, paler and more cupped roses on the breasts of the Vlammalba and those larger, wider-petaled ones that graced the Vlammere), who performed an airborne pirouette and twittered something so rapidly that the girl couldn't catch the individual words.

Hler sang in his clear tenor, "This is Hla, hatchling of Vlin and Vleer, sister-mate of Hliss. She greets you with more questions than you might answer between midsummer and first snow, but she says that the voices from afar have told all in Rhooshal of your coming, and she offers you sister-friendship."

Ila was trying to frame a reply when Hla, with a parting burst of music, hurried forward to fly beside her mother, leaving Ila and Hler to conclude, as her mother had long before, that if any Vla had ever learned to bounce, even in midair, it was Hla.

CHAPTER TWELVE

The Vla were tiring. It was apparent in the slacken-
ing of speed, as well as in the fact that the careless
grace of their usual flight had sunk into a determined effort. The thermals that had favored them
earlier in the day were now failing, and Ila could feel
the *tha-da-dub, tha-da-dub* of Hler's heart vibrating
through his bones. Only twice had they paused, all
that long day, for rest and food, and the girl had
seen that many of the eldest were at the edge of
exhaustion, even unburdened as they were.

She was worrying quietly, as the sun rode down
the western sky, when she felt Hler give a start and
put on a burst of speed. Looking about, she realized
that the entire group was now hurrying forward and
beginning to glide downward toward a table-flat
space on the side of a tremendous peak of rock that
soared upward from that point to hide its top in a
thin layer of cloud.

As those in the lead began to alight, the girl saw
that other groups were approaching from different
angles, and she realized that this was, in truth, a
gathering together of all the Vla. From what she had
understood from Vlin, this was the first time within
memory that the feathered people had come to-

gether, except at the midsummer mating flights. And only in the dim distances of legend had they met at the High Place of Union.

Now Hler cupped his wings to slow his descent, and his passenger heard the whistle of wind through the wing feathers. When his strong toes touched, there was no sound, no feel of impact . . . suddenly Ila found herself set onto the rock, and that was when she realized that they were no longer airborne.

They stood at the very edge of the apron of stone, with the mountain dropping away into darkness at their feet. Night had followed them, and only the peaks behind still glowed with golden light. The gathering of Vla were gilded, and even the Ered were turned into magical gnomes in the unearthly glow.

Ila felt a touch at her shoulder and looked up to see Vlin, her feathers awash in sunfire, looking down at her.

"Come, Ila, and take food. The day has been long, and we must all rest, but I wish for you to know my child, Hla."

Ila chuckled. "We've met, Vlin. Do you know she actually bounces while she flies? Not all the time, of course, but she was talking with you, and we were behind, and when she got excited she just bobbed like a balloon."

"What a balloon is I do not know, but if it resembles Hla, yes, it does bounce. She is a dear Vlammalba, but she can be wearing to the old and weary.

Her enthusiasm is a beautiful thing, and she sings fit to waken the gods to joy, but she is one reason I had gone away into the lowlands where I met you. She . . . she *expects* things of me." And Vlin sighed a sigh so human that Ila was hard put to keep a straight face, though she had no idea if the old Vlammalba had yet learned to decipher human facial expressions.

Suddenly the girl gestured toward an Ered who stood near the spot where Vleer and Kli were still in conference with Alice.

"Isn't that the Ered who first met us and brought you to the hut?" she asked, and Vlin turned to look.

"True, that is he. You have a good eye, child; the Ered are not easy to distinguish, one from the other, except for the Oldest. And for us they have no names, for their own visual patterns for themselves are too intricate for our inner vision to perceive. . . ." But she was talking to the wind, for Ila had darted away and was patting her first friend on Vlahil upon the back and trying to make out what he was trying to ask of her.

"Alice . . . yes, I have that . . . and the wood by the hut . . . the Handmouse? . . . oh! You want music? You would like for Alice to make music so all the Vla and the Ered can hear? Wonderful!" And Ila bent over Alice to ask, "Are you still charged enough to provide music for our new friends, old chum? Or did our two professor-types drain you dry all day?"

"I soaked up sun all day, too," the Companion

reminded her. "I think perhaps this gathering, in this place, waiting to speak with the "gods" at dawn, would find the *Pastoral Symphony* quite appropriate, don't you?"

Ila looked across the miles, where only the edges of the ranges were now faintly gilded and the stars were marching up the sky in unfamiliar multitudes, and she smiled. "Yes, my friend, I do indeed." She called to Vlin, who swept the throng silent with one wing-brush, and then sank to the rock and laid her cheek against Alice's black case.

The joyful first notes of Beethoven's symphony rang out across the throng of alien beings, and a startled movement fluttered across the group. Then they fell silent, as dawn strode up the sky of a deaf musician's Earth, and the enchantment of his invention held them spellbound.

When Alice fell silent, there was a sigh from every throat, and all who had listened stretched and gazed about as though they had slept and dreamed a lovely dream. Vleer and Kli, who had been told of the strange music of the earthlings by Vlin, were all but stricken dumb by its complexity and variety of tonalities.

Ila found it necessary, then and there, to explain the different musical instruments and the sounds they made, as well as she could manage, and she found that the concept of making music using a device was undreamed of among the people of Vlahil.

"Why, with such, the Ered could make their own

music!" exclaimed Kli. "Voicelessness would be no impediment. And even we, who all sing, could enhance our song until the very gods might stop to listen. When we have found our answers and dealt with our problems, Ila, you and your Companion must . . . if you will . . . show us the way to make these marvelous things. Do you think us capable of fashioning them?"

"Anyone who can make the communications system you have, and the air bottles, not to mention many other things I'm sure you have that I know nothing about as yet, can surely shape musical instruments from wood and metal. What I can't help you with, I'm sure Alice can. We can make Vlahil sing from pole to pole!" Ila's eyes were sparkling with enthusiasm, and her cheeks were flushed as she considered the proposal.

But here Vlin firmly quashed further discussion and sent the entire group to their rest. The Vla in their feathers, the Ered in their leathery skins, and Alice in her plastic case were untroubled by the bite of the wind across their high perch, but Ila, even in her coverall and jumper of impenetrable sheenite, found herself shivering, her teeth chattering. Vlin, at the edge of sleep, crouched in the strange attitude of resting Vla, heard that odd clicking, found its source, and assessed its cause in one swift calculation of her mathematician's intellect.

Moving softly, she reached the spot where Ila lay, gathered the girl into the curve of her resting wings, and eased her head into her own downy lap. She hummed a faint melody, and the weary earthling drifted away into sleep, snug in a feather tent composed solely of Vlammalba.

Had any lain awake to watch, the night at that lonely altitude would have taught them the glory of starlight, but none of the exhausted group knew. The winds fingered feathers and caressed Ered-skin, the dim light of the stars washed them in ghostly glow, and the moon, rising late, silvered them impartially, but only when the wind died before dawn did Kli stir and stretch his white wings to their fullest extension.

The notes of the morning song burst from his throat, to echo faintly from distant prominences. And the Vla awoke to song, as had been their habit for millennia beyond remembering. Ila and the Ered sat erect, listening with total attention, as the music gathered momentum, augmented as it was by both the male and female voices. There were no words, but the tones rang with supplication, with joy, with triumph, building to a heart-wrenching climax, sheared suddenly to silence.

Then the gods spoke.

For a time, Ila could not find the source of the organlike voices that vibrated her to her bones. Then, as the dawn light turned the sky to mauve and silver, she saw, as if through a milky window, shapes standing in the sky, against a wavering background that was neither sky nor any world she knew.

Each of the Vla, each of the Ered stood or sat as if turned to stone, listening, she intuited, to a voice that spoke only to it. And in the depths of her own mind the organ tones muted to a quiet level and spoke to her in Euranglo, the tongue of her childhood.

"Greetings, Earth-child," it said quietly. "We have looked long into your dimension, but few have eyes to see or ears to hear us. When we found that even those were derided or considered mad . . . or worse . . . we stilled our tongues and only watched. Here, in this place of Vlahil, there were the Ered, who see with their souls, and we found it easy to teach them the things they needed to learn. They, in turn, taught the Vlammalba and led them to our counsels.

"We speak to each in his own way of the things that concern him. Your heart is open, as you have found in dealing with these of Vlahil, who are so strange to your kind. We can communicate with you, undeterred by the thought of what might happen to you at the hands of your own race. And we have a task for you that is difficult, even dangerous, and that may last for a very long span of time."

Ila listened, her eyes wide in wonder, as the voice spoke softly within her. Now and again she nodded, but she paled as it went on, and there were tears in her eyes when it fell silent.

"It is the only way, I see that," she whispered at last. "But it is a painful thing to know that I must give up these beautiful people. They seem already more akin to me than any on my own world ever did, except for my family."

Then she straightened her shoulders and stead-
ied her voice. "Are you truly gods? I was taught all
my life that there are no gods, just chance combina-
tions and random happenings."

There was a note of amusement in the voice as it
answered, "Not in the way you think of them are we
gods. We are another step nearer the Center of
things than those in your frame of reference. In
some ways the chain of lives is like a ladder, each
dimension one remove up or down with reference
to That Which Is At The Top. Only in a few places
are the dimensions discernible, one to the other, as
here in the High Place of Union.

"There are some who can look across into other
continua from places that exist in their spirits, not
necessarily geographical spots. Many of those live in
madhouses on your home planet.

"In some ways, what we know of the Cosmos is
like a flower, some of whose petals go into invisible
dimensions, but all joined at the center, where the
heart of the flower rests in golden serenity. But that
heart joins the petals together, knows what each one
is like, and holds the blossom in a coherent shape.

"We are one step up the ladder . . . or one petal
fragment nearer the Center . . . from this particular state of being. There are those who teach us, as
we teach the Ered and the Vla, and many other races
besides those. If gods are the Powers of Tyranny
and Destruction, then we are not gods; but if, to
you, gods are those who teach what we need to
learn, then we may seem so."

The voice stilled, and Ila looked away into the distances that rolled to the edge of sight. Peaks to the east were outlined in gold, while those in the west were glowing with pale pink as the sun climbed over the ranges. The world of the "gods" had faded to a flicker of light and shadow against the sky, but the sense of their presence was strong and clear.

"I will do what I must, for my own people and for the people of Vlahil," she said at last. "But can you give me hope that I may return here, sometime, to work and live with the Vla? Maybe even to learn to sing with them?"

"Have no fear, Ila. You will not lose them, nor must you leave them very soon. There is much to do before the troubles of Vlahil may come to an end."

The girl felt a gentle withdrawal, and something in her tried to cling to the presence that had filled her mind, but it was inexorable. Emptied at last, she stood and looked at the multitude upon the rock. They were stretching, standing, looking about, just as she was doing. And about each there was an aura of joy that was almost a color, almost a sound, almost, indeed, an inaudible music.

CHAPTER THIRTEEN

The Handmouse watched. Of all the creatures in the forest, that small being was the most curious, the most daring in the pursuit of its curiosity. For all the spans of time, and they were very long, since the Ered had completed the taming of the continent, the Handmice had observed their fellow creatures with lively interest, the Ered with as much reverence as lay in their characters, and the distantly swooping Vla with frustration.

Now there were new beasts in the forest, and there were new ways among the old beasts that lived there. With terror, the Handmice learned that their old security was no longer valid, that there were those among even their own companions of old, such as the Spiderbeasts, that would hunt them down and eat their flesh, though food of other nature was still abundant.

When the Ered had laid the calming influence of their minds upon the beasts, they had found that, of them all, only one species had no murderous impulses. The Handmice were wary and intelligent, good at hiding and slipping, unseen, through the lower ways of a wood, but they killed no meat for their food. Even in defending themselves and their young, they killed only when no other way was possible. They were very near the thin line dividing sapient creatures from mere animals, and the Ered, in their patient, unstressful way, were leading them nearer that line in every generation.

So the Handmouse that watched the Earthlings was far more than one more beast in a wood. He knew that the Ered would come, perhaps even the Vla. He realized that the creatures in the shell of metal were alien to his environment, though it is doubtful if any of his folk had yet looked up at the stars with speculation.

The Earthlings were moving about in their shell. He could hear occasional clankings and thuddings as they carried on their mysterious activities. When the hatch slid open and the figures, no longer suited, as they had found the planet safe, clambered down the ladder, the Handmouse crouched lower in his hidden place, but he continued to watch.

They came out armed with their weapons, and the Handmouse knew that they were again ready to hunt, for he had seen the slaying of many of his kind in the days since the craft had landed. Upon the tenuous web of contact that stretched, mind-to-mind, among his kind in the immediate area, he sent out a hasty warning: *Hide! The slayers walk! Hide yourselves!*

For a time, they busied themselves about their campsite. Then, taking up the weapons again, they went away into the wood, and the Handmouse, greatly daring, even for his kind, ventured out into that open spot and scuttered about, examining with sensitive nose, discerning eyes, and tiny hands anything that he could reach. There were many metal objects that he surveyed closely. There was a pit, from which the stench quickly drove him, chittering with dismay, but which he observed to be filled with skins and offal from the prey the beings had killed in the wood thereabout.

He did not venture into the shell. It had a terrifying strangeness to it, a smell unlike anything he had ever known, and even his driving curiosity could not send him into it. Yet he was near enough to sapience, well enough taught by the Ered, to etch into his memory the symbols painted in white against the dark-gray side of the craft.

A sound from the forest brought him to his full fourteen-inch height, round, furry ears twitching, hands folded sedately across his paunchy belly. Then, with a nervous squeak, he dashed for cover, found his hidden track in the undergrowth, and scurried for his burrow.

But in his capaciously rounded skull a great deal of information was safely stored, against future need.

CHAPTER FOURTEEN

Vleer felt the chill of the high places in his bones, even beneath his snowy feathers. His discomfort was such that he urged haste upon Vlin and Kli and the aeries of Rhoosh and Rhooshal, and before the sun was well above the mountain peaks, the three had conferred with their fellow elders and were airborne on their homeward flight.

The Vla were still weary, for one night's rest was not enough to restore their strength after so long a flight, burdened as they had been with the Ered, Ila, and Alice. Ila could sleep against Hler's feathery and keellike breast, and the Ered, most of them, did likewise.

Vleer, Vlin, and Kli, with Alice, flew again in a tight formation, close enough for conversation, and Kli held the Oldest Ered. Ila could hear, in her brief moments of waking, the musical conversation taking place so near, but she was too weary and too bemused with her communication with the "gods" to attend very closely.

The day wore on, and the sun disappeared behind banks of cloud that pursued it from the eastern reaches of the sky. A chill drizzle began, the first rain Ila had seen on Vlahil, and it wearied the struggling

Vla even more. At last, the peaks of Rhooshal loomed before them through the mists, and Vleer's voice called out, "Rest upon the ledges of Rhooshal, my children. It is not a customary thing to do, but these are times that challenge custom. Rest, and put down your passengers."

With relief, the Vlammere and the Vlammalba found spots upon balconies and ledges and rested their weary wings from flight. And after a short time of trillings and melodic consultations all the passengers were brought to a large balcony and ushered into the meeting hall of Rhooshal.

Ila thanked her faithful bearer, but she realized that he hardly heard her as she spoke. He was looking past her toward the group of Vlammalba who stood welcoming their visitors into the arched portal. His eyes held an almost glazed look, and she knew that his strong Vla heart had been racing when he set her down. Now she realized that its strange pulsations had not been caused entirely by the exertions of the day.

When she entered the doorway, she realized that Hler was not alone in his bemusement. The young Vlammalba who greeted her twittered welcomes sincerely, but their eyes and their thoughts were with the Vlammere, who remained on the balcony, sheltered from the rain but exposed to the chill wind that sang among the heights.

Ila found Vlin settling her charges on large baglike cushions, directing distracted Vlammalba to bring food and drink, and checking frequently on the Oldest Ered, who lay on her cushion, evidently too exhausted even to take nourishment. Making her way to the Oldest's side, Ila said to Vlin, "You have so much to do . . . let me watch her. When she is able I'll feed her some of the broth they are bringing in those big bowls. She'll be all right; she's just tired, I think."

Vlin looked at the girl, and the slight twitch at the corner of her eyelid that served as a smile made itself known.

"Tend her, then, Ila, and I will make certain that all is well among the rest of our guests." She turned with a flutter of wings and was gone across the great hall, pausing now and again to commune with an Ered or one of her own folk.

When the Oldest Ered woke from her light sleep, she was weary indeed, and Ila could see, even in that alien face, the traces of shadow that might mean death. Concerned, the girl coaxed the old Ered to sip broth, nibble a bit of the nutty bread that the Vla so loved, but that shadow did not fade.

"Talk with me, Oldest," she said at last. "I know it is hard for you, but I am so curious about your world and all the people on it."

The dry rustle of the Ered's mind-voice whispered to her, "Oh, child, Vlahil has become a weariness to me and all its folk a burden. Death calls me strongly, and I am sorely tempted to go, needful though my service may be to all those here. Talk to me, instead, of your own place and its ways."

Ila was silent for a moment, thinking deeply.

Then she stood. "My world is not a cheerful thing, now, for one who is tempted by death. But it has begotten many things of joy and beauty, and I will show you one of them." She walked away into the depths of the chamber and knelt beside Alice, interrupting a conversation between that black-cased lady and her two Vlammere admirers.

"Forgive me," she said, "but I must borrow Alice for a bit. The Oldest is very weak and terribly tired, and I think she needs something new to waken her interest." She bent and lifted Alice and bore her away to the Oldest Ered's side.

"What waltzes do you have?" she asked, and Alice's toplight flickered for a moment, then she answered, "Many, but how about the *Eugen Onegin?*"

"Alice, you have perfect taste and judgment. Of course. What a pity you're not presently able to waltz with me."

The toplight flashed brightly as the Companion chuckled, "Don't think I couldn't have, back when I had feet to dance with. But why not ask an Ered? The Vla are too tall, and their wings would get in the way, but an Ered would do quite well."

Ila gazed about until she saw her own original Ered, who was lying at ease, mopping up his broth with a bit of bread. She went to him, bent, and laid her hand on his shoulder. Startled, he looked up, then rose to face her.

With careful precision, Ila pictured in her mind an Ered waltzing, drawing in as well as she could the steps, the motion, the swirling rhythm of the dance.

Then, difficult as it was, she added herself to the picture, and suddenly it grew easier. In her mind she could see herself and the Ered dancing, and she realized that the small being had grasped the idea and was helping her with the imagery. Laughing, she held out her hands, and the Ered took them.

Alice, with perfect timing, began the lilting waltz, and, as the chamber full of Ered and Vlammalba watched with astonishment, Ila and the Ered swung into the dance. It was as if all the hunger for music, for things beautiful, that was in his kind responded to the melody and the motion, for moment by moment the Ered became more proficient. Ila, always a joyful dancer, found that the peculiar empathic sense of her partner allowed them to do the most difficult maneuvers with polished ease, and they dipped and swooped about the chamber until it seemed as if they, like the Vla, were on the verge of flight.

The others in the room formed a wide circle, watching closely without impeding their performance. And many of the Ered in that circle began, as if unconsciously, to move about in their places, echoing the rhythms, imitating the motions.

When the waltz was done and the two dancers stood panting in the center of the circle, the Oldest rose, though with some effort, and made her way to them.

She put her hands on either side of Ila's face and looked into her eyes. The voice whispered again in the Earthling's mind, "Oh, child! You have given us

a precious gift. Never had any on our world, save
only those who fly, known this sort of movement-to-
music. It makes me young again to see, to hear, to
feel it. You must teach us all to dance!''

Ila looked about her, feeling the imploring gaze
of those dozens of Ered. She felt a presence at her
elbow, and Vlin stood there, nodding her regal
head.

"Never have we seen such a joyful thing, Ila.
Teach the Ered, that we may watch them with the
same joy with which they have always listened to our
singing."

"Gladly," said Ila. "But I need something—
scarves? Ribbons? Something silken and swirly to
drape on the Ered. Then you will have something
really lovely to watch."

Vlin gave a musical call, and several of the
younger Vlammalba flew from the chamber into the
wide arched corridor at its back. In a short time they
returned, bearing in their arms strips of light and
gauzy material in delicate colors. With Ila's help,
they began draping it about the leathery shoulders
of the Ered, who seemed a little embarrassed at such
unaccustomed finery. They soon were beguiled by
the beauty of the stuff, nevertheless, and they
turned about, watching it flow across the air behind
them.

It was a strange dancing lesson. Ila stood in the
middle of a circle of Ered, holding her partner's
hand. They both projected the motions of the
dance, the very sensation of the muscles in the dif-

ferent steps and spins. Their pupils were apt, for
soon they broadcast a rosy glow of approval that
meant they were ready to try their new art.

Alice, noting the flowerlike colors of their new
adornments, played the "Waltz of the Flowers," and
the room dissolved into a kaleidoscope of rippling
forms and colors as the Ered danced. It seemed as
though the short, clumsy beings they had been had
metamorphosed into bright and graceful creatures
that danced like feathers on the wind.

Ila, watching between Vlin and the Oldest Ered,
felt almost intoxicated. Turning to speak to Vlin,
she found her in the same state, standing on tiptoe,
swaying with the music, her wings half unfolded, as
though she were about to take wing. Then she did
take wing and flew out into the space above
Rhooshal, and the Vlammere and the Vlammalba
followed her. Then they all began to sing, their
wordless music matching harmonies and tempi with
that of Tchaikovsky with impeccable musicianship.
They danced in the sky, a storm of white feathery
forms in an aerobatic ballet, while the Ered danced
on within Rhooshal.

Ila, left beside the Oldest Ered, could see both the
inner and the outer dancers. No fantasy in all her life
had ever approached the heart-wrenching glory of
this strange festival, and she found tears in her eyes.
Then she felt the Oldest move beside her, and that
hard, warm little hand was again laid on her shoulder.

"Sleep, child," she said. "You have given me new

life and my people a way to ease their hearts. Rest, for they will dance until they can dance no more. Sleep."

And, with familiar and alien music in her ears, Ila slept.

CHAPTER FIFTEEN

It rained for many days, making the journey from Rhooshal to Rhoosh a wet and chilly one. And even the comfortable halls of Rhoosh seemed a little dank, the light within them dimmed, when Ila found herself again in the apartments of Vleer and Kli. Even after the obliging Ered (her own Ered, she thought of him) had chiseled her a living-space of her own, decorated with a quiet pattern of intertwining ferns, she felt depressed.

"I'm missing Vlin," she finally admitted to Alice, who, for once, was not busy with the elders.

"I don't wonder. Vleer and Kli are estimable creatures, but neither of them is the slightest bit motherly," the Companion said dryly. "Then, too, you are waiting for your task to begin. If you had something to keep you busy, you'd be as happy as I am."

Ila thunked her fingernail against the black case. "You know Vlin didn't spoil me! And she's not a bit like my mother! But you're right, I do need something to do."

"It won't be long. The Vlammere are hatching up something with the Ered, and they will need you to carry it out. They have gotten—somehow that is beyond me—the serial number of the scout ship.

I've given them everything I know about that model."

"Is there *anything* that you don't know something about?" Ila asked, amused. "I have yet to ask you for anything that you can't provide."

"When you live as long as I lived and read everything and watch every tape you can get your hands on and are a *librarian*, and when you have an eidetic memory wedded to the molecular-imprint capabilities of a computer, my child, you have just about everything somewhere within you," Alice replied loftily. "Besides, scout ships were one of my hobbies. I knew every one they made after the DEF-Sequence from stem to stern. If I could have figured a way to take all the books I had never read with me, I might very likely have been one of a scout team."

The girl patted the shiny case. "Well, you finally made it off-planet, didn't you, even if you didn't get a ship to do it in?"

The rustle of wings interrupted them, and Kli fluttered into the room, followed by Vleer and the Oldest Ered.

"Greetings, Ila," whispered the Ered's voice in her mind. "We have a task for you. Are you ready?"

"More than ready, since Vlin is working in Rhooshal to build up the energy reserves. What do you want me to do?"

Ila climbed on the tall stool they had permanently installed for her and looked into the feathery faces that were now level with her own. From an adjoining stool, the Oldest Ered smiled at her and gestured toward Vleer.

"We have found that the Ered cannot reach into the minds of those in the south," he said. "They are unreachable by any technique they know. Even the Oldest is unable to pierce the fog of noise and chaos that surrounds their mental processes. Yet we know that they must be stopped from slaying the happy beasts. They must kill no more Ered. We can only agree to one thing, since the gods affirmed that we should not soil our world with the blood of outlanders. They must be stilled for a time, while one who knows their artifacts disarms them and their vessel. Can you do this for us?"

Ila nodded. "This is the first—and the least—of the tasks I was given at the High Place of Union. But it is far, so Vlin told me, to the place where they are. Can the Vla carry me so great a distance?"

"There will be no need," answered Kli. "We have a way of travel that we seldom use, for there is little need on Vlahil for such speed. But there are times when need arises, and for these occasions the *klin* was devised and tested and stored against future necessity. When all is ready, you will be transported instantly into the forest near the ship of your fellow beings. It was for that purpose that Vlin remained in Rhooshal, for it is upon the heights that the energy collectors are placed, and she must see that all is fully charged. Much is required for the operation of the klin."

"Instantaneous matter transmission?" Ila asked,

with intense interest. "It is by that method that I came to Vlahil. And my folk believe that there is no intelligent life here!"

Alice chuckled. "I have an idea that the Ered and the Vla, between them, have more useful gadgets, fully understood and controlled, than Earth ever had or dreamed of. They have sense enough to use their machines, instead of allowing the machines to use them . . . though that may sound a bit strange, coming from me."

Ila laughed aloud, the Vla crinkled their eye-corners, and the Oldest Ered bathed them all in orange bursts of amusement. Then they grew sober, as they outlined their plan of action.

So it was that, on the third day after, Ila found herself standing in the meeting hall at Rhooshal, looking out over a multitude of feathery shapes of Vlammere and Vlammalba and numbers of the Ered. The Ered lay on the baglike pillows (Vlin had explained that they held the molted down from the members of the aeries; the Vla wasted nothing), and each was surrounded by a circle of Vla.

The hall was silent—more silent than any gathering of Vla the girl had yet seen. The concentration of mind and energy that filled the place was almost visible, as the Ered closed their eyes and focused their minds on the beings in the south. As they built the strength of their projection, sustained by the physical energy the Vla poured into them, Ila found herself able to see the working-out of their project.

Into her mind came a vision of the clearing in the

forest, the shape of the scout ship, the forms of two human beings, a man and a woman, sitting on crudely hacked stumps beside the entry ramp. About that scene, she could sense the forming of a bubble of force. The sunlight within dimmed a bit, as if the almost invisible barrier shut out some of its rays. The wind breathed through, for she could see the grasses moving, but a flying insect shot away at a tangent, as it encountered the obstacle.

The tension in the meeting hall eased, and it seemed as if all the participants relaxed for a moment, to rest and draw upon fresh energies. Then a different sort of force began building, and Ila felt her eyes grow heavy, her head begin to droop, until Vlin held the air bottle under her nose and brought her to herself with a draught of oxygen.

"They will sleep, now," the Vlammalba breathed into her ear. "They will sleep for many hours, taking no harm, but allowing you to go and come without stress for them or for you. Come, now, to your place. It is time."

About them, the others were beginning to move, to stretch their tired muscles and unkink their aching bones. Many of the Ered had drifted into sleep of their own, there on the pillows. For the next step belonged to the Vla, and to Ila.

It had never occurred to the girl that the Vla needed no stairways, until she followed Vlin out into the arched hallway and saw the shafts leading up and down into the many levels of Rhooshal. But Kli, behind her, touched her shoulder and she accepted his aid as he lifted her and spiraled up the wide, brightly lit well that seemed to open into the free air of the heights but was, she saw as they neared the top, closed with a transparent dome. Before reaching that, her companions swooped to light on a shell-curved lip of stone that led into a small bright chamber.

Ila looked about in awe. Remembering the sterile ugliness of the Transfer, she was ashamed of the uncultured race from which she sprang. The room was like the inside of a pearl, the walls mistily opalescent. Conduits were webbed over the entire surface, but they were burnished silver and arranged in patterns of startling beauty, though not an extra inch had been used. The innate artistry of the Vla, wedded to their technical mastery, had made of a device a thing, also, of loveliness.

In the center of the room was a scalloped platform of the silver metal. Above it was a canopy that matched its shape, curve for curve. Attaching the two were light rods of a different material that connected the outward curves at their centers.

Into the airy cage the Vla conducted Ila. Then Vlin went to a complex of silver shapes on the wall and touched one, two, three, in an intricate and repetitious pattern. At once, the rods about Ila began a humming that was almost out of hearing range. She felt, once again, the universe quiver . . . and stood elsewhere.

About her, the forest murmured with life. She looked about and realized that she had been set just

within the bubble that the Ered had fixed about the
scout ship. The two Earthlings slept where they had
slumped from their seats, and she looked closely at
them.

They were very young, she realized. She felt as
though her own twenty-five years must be ancient
beside their vulnerable youth. Their hands were
grubby, and the girl had gone to sleep with the
traces of tears upon her cheeks. They were no vil-
lains, these two, only other hapless victims of the
terrible and inhuman logic of the Instrumentality.

She sighed. Then she stooped to pick a pale-pink
blossom from the stub of the flowering vine they
had hacked away, and she laid it in the girl's half-
open hand.

She went up the ramp without caution. She
doubted that they had set any booby traps, and she
was uncertain that she could detect them if they had.
She trusted that the "gods" knew what they were
doing when they gave her her instructions. The inside of the ship was a mess. These children, she felt
certain, must be the products of the public crèches
that the Instrumentality had so fervently fostered.
No one with any concept of a home or decent living
could have tolerated such conditions.

But the weapons were easily found. Solar-powered lasers she had expected, but the ugly, com-
pressed-air handguns that fired knurled slugs were
new to her. For what purpose had the powers-that-
be provided such equipment? Then she realized
that the Instrumentality considered any life forms

encountered on other worlds as either specimens or game.

The ship's built-in weapons system was controlled by a central computer, which she proceeded to burn out with one of the lasers. Then she went outside and welded shut their nozzles. That left the awkward pile of portable weapons to dispose of. Finally, she fused them into a mass of metal and molten plastic with the last of the laser rifles. That done, she went through the ship again, searching every corner for anything lethal she might have missed, but she found nothing more.

At last, she took the last rifle and went to the spot at which she had arrived. Knowing that she had been watched by the Ered all the while, she waited confidently, though she did not quite understand how the mechanism could return her to Rhooshal without having an extension here where she stood.

Vlin had explained the device's affinity for molecules that had passed through it, its limited-span-enduring field, but Ila had lacked the patience, at that moment, to absorb it all. Nevertheless, she felt again that disruption of the universe and found herself back upon the platform in the bright chamber at Rhooshal.

Vlin ran her fingers up a conduit, down another, and the hum died from the rods. Ila stepped down and handed the rifle to Kli, who took it gingerly and with distaste.

"The Ered will provide fruits and grains for them now," said Alice. "Vleer has been telling me that they won't be able to leave the force-field until it is decided what to do with them. But they won't suffer because of that. The Ered have a way of damping the field for short periods in small areas, so they can put things inside.

"And right now, the Ered and most of the Vla are back at work, adding to the field around them, so that their mental emanations can't escape and set the animals to killing one another again. They have been sent to Coventry. And, while you were busy with the weaponry, the Oldest drew from their minds all that they knew and stored it in me. You'll be dealing with them, Ila, so you must know them from stem to stern. That will be our project for some time to come."

Ila patted Alice's case. "Tomorrow, old girl. Tomorrow." She went gratefully with Vlin to a side chamber, where she sank into a down-filled bag and was asleep instantly.

But, inexorably, the morning came. Ila found herself strangely nervous about the linkage with the minds of her fellow Terrans.

"The culture, if you can call it that, that the Instrumentality has created is as sterile and uncreative as it can be made. Any attempt at originality or individuality is stamped out as soon as it can be detected. Only the very wealthy and powerful, such as my own father, succeed in shielding themselves and their children from the system. I suppose you could say that I'm afraid something of the mind-limiting techniques of the Instrumentality may rub off on me," she said to Vlin and Alice, as they prepared for the project.

Vlin touched her cheek with a snowy wing tip. "Alice has told us of your concern," she trilled. "There are few dangers in such linkage, we feel, but the Oldest Ered will attend you to safeguard your mind from contamination, if it should seem necessary. She is coming with several of the other Ered through the Ered-passages that twist through the walls of Rhooshal, giving that wingless folk access to all levels."

Reassured, Ila again accepted the offices of young Hler, who lifted her and bore her across the well beneath the dome to another balcony. By the time Ila, Kli, Vlin, and Vleer reached the room where the attempt was to be made, the Oldest was waiting for them.

This was a larger chamber than that across the way, and it was fitted out with complexities of conduits, gauges, and what could only be dials that made those of the room across the way look simple. Preoccupied as she was, Ila found herself drawn to the strange dials. Here there were no flavorless white faces with numbers and pointing hands. Instead, there were iridescent discs that glowed in every shade of the spectrum, each variation of color denoting a particular phenomenon, flux, or state of being in the system monitored. With a sigh, she left the curving wall that flowered with light, and Vlin led her to a chair that must have been created specifically for her by the Vla and the Ered.

The chair provided cushioned support for arms, legs, and head. No distracting friction could Ila feel. She looked up from her semi-reclining position and saw hanging above her a curving bell, almost like a gigantic dish cover.

"Aha!" she commented to Alice. "A sensory-deprivation tank. That should make things much easier."

Alice's toplight flashed agreement, as the Vla began the intricate series of hookups that would feed the sensory data gleaned by the Oldest Ered and stored in the computer directly into Ila's consciousness. When they were done, Vlin laid her hand on Ila's forehead for a brief moment, and the girl felt her eyes grow heavy. She saw the tank above her begin its descent, the light grow dimmer until there was nothing but blackness, and then her world disappeared entirely, and she swam in the strange seas of another's identity.

CHAPTER SIXTEEN

Jir crouched behind the metal dome, shivering. The door was sealed to her, she knew . . . perhaps forever, if she could not complete her assignment. Though the Nans in the crèche had taught her carefully everything in their programs, and though they had assured her that she was fully capable of killing a fluun without being killed first, she was terribly afraid.

But the day was passing. She knew that there was no possibility of anyone's surviving a night outdoors on Ra, for even a Nan, left outside as an experiment, had been found the next morning in a tangle of metal limbs and jumbled wiring. Her only course was to get the thing over with, one way or the other, as soon as could be.

She went sunward, across the burningly green savanna that stretched away on all sides of the crèche. After a few strides, she was neck-deep in the grasses that almost swallowed up her four-year-old stature. The specially built laser rifle she carried, as she had been taught, at the ready. Inwardly, she rehearsed her teaching: "Any beast encountered is potentially deadly. Take no chance; shoot to kill, even though it may not seem immediately threatening." But she was frightened, frightened to the depths of her soul, and she knew that she would never again be without something of that all-trembling fear.

Her short legs grew weary very soon, for the grasses hampered every step, and she had to force a passage through them. The weapon, small though it was, grew unbearably heavy. At last, tired and hungry, she waded out of the grass onto a rocky outcrop that footed a hillock crowned with scrubby trees. Making her way to the top, she dropped onto short turf and looked about, searching each quarter of the compass thoroughly before she relaxed.

Then she grinned, a small, impish smirk. Knowing the ways of the crèche with the infallibility of an observing child, she had been forewarned that she would be given no food for the day. But bit-by-bit pilferings from her own plate over the past two days had given her a store of rations that she had concealed in her trouser leg and secured with her boot top.

Hunger appeased, Jir lay on the little hilltop, keeping close watch on the surrounding savanna. No one who was unfamiliar with the techniques used in the Instrumentality crèches would have believed the complexity of her mental processes. She was assessing her chances of survival, not only on the hunt, but also after her return to the crèche.

She well knew that only the brightest and most inquisitive of the children were required to make the fluun-hunt. And that relatively few of those ever returned from it. Those few she knew to be watched closely by both the Nans and the dreaded Assessors. Some were taken away, never to be spoken of again. Those who were allowed to remain were very quiet, very guarded.

Only the ones who returned so shaken and shocked by their day outside that they seemed stupid and tractable were allowed to live unmonitored. The child nodded slowly, her black eyes sparkling with determination. She would kill her fluun. Or, if she did not, it would kill her, and there would be no more problem. If she returned, she would return to babyhood, like Lis and Jay. They would carefully teach her to speak again, to feed herself, to read the parts manuals and the skills-instructions on machinery.

It would be easy to fool the Nans. And, once she had convinced the primary Assessor, she need not fear being brought before it a second time . . . unless she made a foolish mistake.

She stood, then, and looked carefully about. Then she made her way back to the grasses and slid into them, weapon charged.

The fluun came like a projectile, whistling through the tangled grasses, its steam-kettle cries rousing flaps of seed-birds from the savanna. Jir dropped where she was, twisted onto her back, and beamed the Airedale-sized beast as it overshot her position. It hit with a thump, and a last shrill gasp was forced from its dead lungs. Jir wriggled through the grass, adjusted the beam of her rifle, and neatly severed the thing's ears. They were her passport back into the crèche, if she could reach it alive.

Ra being a small planet, the sun was well down the sky before Jir stood again beside the dome. She took the prickly furred ears from her boot top and dropped them, one at a time, into the slot beside the sealed door. There was a long wait. The sun dipped lower, until its edge was touching the rippling savanna. Jir huddled against the door, hugging her knees, and the fear surrounded her like a chill web.

Darkness began to spread across the grasslands, and still there was no reply from the crèche. The sun was gone, and only its last afterglow lit the world. A subtle change was coming over the lands, and a dim twittering sound began to punctuate the dimness. Jir felt unseen eyes boring into her back, but nothing was to be seen, though she stood and turned slowly, her finger on the firing stud of her weapon.

The day had been long, full of terror, loneliness, and danger. Jir was, for all her tough fiber and excellent mind, a four-year-old. As the invisible menace of the darkness drew close about her, she began to cry, the desolate wail of an infant left too long alone. And, just as the darkness was becoming absolute, the door slid into its niche, with a hiss, letting a stream of cold white light slash across the night.

In a turmoil of exhausted hysteria, the child was lifted and carried into the dome by hard, chilly hands. Warm gruel was put into her mouth, though she was almost asleep. She was shaken into wakefulness enough to perform the obligatory washing-up, and then she staggered to her sleeping-capsule and was overtaken by a tide of irresistible unconsciousness.

The night was filled with dreams, but the core of self-preservation that had sustained her through the day sealed them off, so that, when she was awakened, she had no memory of them. Her first moment of wakefulness was filled with triumph. The second diminished to care and caution. She knew that she must show to the Nans and, later, to the primary Assessor a child crushed into numbed submissiveness by the stresses of the hunting day. Only that could save her from whatever fate had overtaken those others whom she had seen succeed and return filled with excited confidence. She had heard other, older children whisper that their brains had been taken to serve as computers of machinery too complex for readily and cheaply manufactured mechanical components. Jir did not intend to spend the next thousand years rumbling across the airless moons of Ra, digging and processing ores.

She lay still, listening intently. When the stolid clunk of a Nan's flat metal feet moved toward her capsule, she began to moan and mutter softly and unintelligibly. She tossed her arms about in an uncoordinated way, and when the Nan appeared above the tall lip of the capsule, she shrank away and began to sob. Squinching her eyes tightly, she hiccuped and wept and let her nose run onto her chin without mopping it. She felt the Nan assessing and recording her reactions, and she didn't even venture to peep in order to judge the effect she was having.

After a time, the Nan reached into the capsule and pushed her down onto her back. The cold fingers stuck an electrode to a spot on her shaven skull, and Jir knew that next a switch would be touched, filling her mind with alpha waves. With a final shudder, the child allowed the soothing rhythms to take over. She opened her eyes and looked up at the Nan with what she hoped was the blank and bemused expression she had seen on the faces of Lis and Jay.

There was a click of satisfaction from the Servo, and the waves were turned off. Jir was lifted out of the capsule and crammed into a jumpsuit and boots. Then the Nan hurried her off down the one corridor that not even the most unruly of the crèche children ever invaded. Cold shivers of apprehension ran up and down her arms and legs. Her stomach seemed filled with cold lumps. But she held on to her blank expression. If she had ever been exposed to any sort of religious thought, she would have prayed, but as it was, she simply trusted to luck and walked without faltering beside the Nan.

The Assessor had no office. It *was* an office, of a sort. Jir had never seen it, for she was by nature cautious as well as observant, but she knew that it was the most sophisticated computer on Ra. When she stood in the center of the circular space that was the interior of the Assessor, she saw about her a multitude of unfamiliar mechanisms. And before her, placed there, no doubt, by some stubborn human holdout in the early days of the Instrumentality, was a kindly and rosy face.

"Come near, child," it said in dulcet tones. "Your name is Jir?"

She stood her ground and let her mouth drop open. Though her knees shook beneath her, she held on to that stubborn core that insisted on being herself. She let a drop of spittle dribble from the corner of her mouth and drool down her chin.

The face frowned a well-tempered frown and said, "You must come near me, Jir. I need to know what happened to you yesterday. Most of your playmates are happy when they complete the hunt. Why are you frightened?"

There was a moment of dizziness before the child realized that the circle about her had shrunk until she was all but touching the surrounding mechanisms. A pistonlike arm shot out and clamped a pressure-cuff about her upper arm. Another sprayed an injection into her other shoulder. Things touched her, measuring, probing, assessing.

Jir almost panicked. For a moment she stood as if paralyzed. Then she took hold of the part that was Jir and willed it away into darkness. With all her strength, she pushed herself away from herself, down a long black tunnel of unconsciousness. With a last instant of awareness, she felt herself slipping toward the floor, with a tangle of tubing and wiring slowing her fall.

She woke in her sleeping-capsule. The wiring had been implanted, instead of the old method of stick-on electrodes being used. She lay in a doze, letting the auto-teacher re-instruct her in the things she had not forgotten. It occurred to her that she had chosen a terribly hard way. To live out the role she had chosen, she must never make a slip, never forget to look and to be stupid but trainable.

The next days were terrible. She relearned from one or another of the Nans how to wash herself, feed herself, even to toilet-train herself. She walked like a Servo, spoke not at all, and could not interact with the other children for fear of betraying herself. That part of her that had been Jir she did not allow to return totally up that dark tunnel down which she had sent it. But she listened.

She could not afford to think. The capsule would have picked up unusual brain activity and it would have meant a return to the Assessor . . . or, even worse, a visit to the Sifter. She was confined within that tunnel inside herself, and it grew instinctive to allow only a fraction of herself to peep forth from it. But she had been a fantastically bright child. Her hearing was acute, and she was considered to be, now, all but mindless.

Her elders, the Nans, the lesser Servos made their observations, their comments, and, the human ones, their complaints as if she were not there at all. And she listened. Not a word escaped her, no innuendo, whether she understood it or not, was lost. All descended that interior tunnel and was stored, along with her lost self, behind the locked panels of her self-control.

CHAPTER SEVENTEEN

Ila floated up from the stream of memory that had borne her along its drift. Through her eyelids, she could see light return, and she knew that the tank had been raised. She opened her eyes, sat up, and stretched.

Vlin bent over her with a flowerlike glass cup in her hand. "Take broth," she sang softly. "Living within the being of another takes toll of the strength. Drink, now, and rest a bit."

Ila accepted the cup and drained it, but she was obsessed by her experience. "Alice," she said to her black-cased Companion, "did you know about the crèches before now? Did anyone have an idea what goes on there?"

The Companion clicked for a moment, then said, "In my life, no, I had no idea beyond what I was told, along with the rest of our race, by the Instrumentality. Ra was said to be 'the playground world,' a small, safe planet where those infants chosen by the Instrumentality were reared in a paradise of warm sunshine, beautiful green meadows, and complete security, attended by the best human and mechanical nurses and teachers that could be attained. 'The new human race' was to grow from these children, reared without stresses or traumas, by the most advanced and psychologically sound methods ever used with human young."

"I kept hearing from people who should have known better," Ila said bitterly, "that the Instrumentality, being now totally computerized, could not lie. Who programmed those computers, Alice? Did they know what they were doing? Was it deliberate?"

Alice's toplight flashed. "Much of it was done by educated fools who wanted to prove theories and hypotheses that any normal six-year-old could have realized were untenable. But you must remember also that the people who rule worlds are usually insatiable egotists. They believe that they should live—and rule—forever. What was done with my own persona was quite possibly done with others, at their own insistence. For myself, I left my body to science, never guessing that those I trusted would betray my trust to the point of stealing my essential self. But those others could have stamped their own biased egos onto the systems that run the galaxies we have overrun.

"That would explain the worst villainies of the Instrumentality, the occasional astounding illogic of some of its methods. Computers cannot lie. I know because, basically, I am one. But my persona is so strong that it can, at times, warp the material I emit in ways that could deceive some people in some circumstances. And I was a fundamentally truthful person."

"So the whole system we knew consists of the permanently pickled prejudices of a few egomaniacs who happened to be in positions of power at a crucial and pivotal time," Ila said.

"I strongly suspect it," Alice replied. "I have wondered and watched and built up theories and destroyed them as I used to keep my eye on the workings of the system. Since I have been, so to speak, disembodied, no one has asked my considered opinion of the situation until now, and I find that my computer system contains much material that makes sense of what used to be deepest conundrum. I must tell you, also, that Ra was only the first, not the only, crèche. There are thousands more, scattered among small, inhabitable planets with no assets that might tempt close scrutiny."

Ila cursed with heartfelt sincerity. Vlin, though the words meant nothing to her, was deeply shocked by their tone and laid her hand on the girl's shoulder.

"You feel deeply, Ila, but do not rend yourself. You cannot undo what has already been done . . . but you may, in future, alter what will be done. Take this perversion of your race's future to the gods. They see around the obstacles that seem impenetrable to us. They always help, though sometimes the results of their workings are only apparent after generations. You will have opportunity to feel their presence again. But now you should rest, for there is another past into which you must go." Vlin took the cup and flitted away to refill it.

Alice, without being asked, said, "She is right, you know. The gods are something that the Instrumentality never suspected existed."

Ila looked at her Companion with surprise. "Did you feel their presence, too? I wouldn't have thought they'd have been apparent to . . ."

"A computer?" Alice ended the sentence for her. "Oh, yes. They spoke to me also. They are real, in their way. More so than we are, I would estimate, for they are not limited to a single set of physical dimensions. They communicated directly with me, without actual words. The concepts they fed into my banks of molecules would have been incomprehensible to me in my former state, for I had not the ability of infinite overlay that the computer system gives me. They told me things that I will only be able to tell you when you lose the limitations of a physical brain and become an energy system."

Ila rubbed her forehead with a weary hand. "I'm not certain I fully understand what you're telling me right now," she said. "I thought, way back in my mind someplace, that what I experienced on that mountain was to a large extent a sort of mass illusion. Even knowing the way I felt afterward, I couldn't square it with all I'd been taught, all my life. But if those . . . beings . . . could communicate with you, I'll have to accept them at face value and go from there. Wow! I wish I could talk to Pup for a week or two. He'd be triumphant to find out that the old-fashioned, outmoded ideas he was derided for all his adult life were aimed in the right direction, after all."

"My acquaintance with your father was of short duration," Alice said, "but I was impressed by the clarity of his mental processes and the originality of his thinking. The educational systems of the Unholy I hadn't made a dent in his intelligence. He reared you as nearly free of that sort of thing as was possible . . . and safe for you. I have thought, since we met, that he had an underlying intention, perhaps even a subconscious one, that you might free yourself of the prison that Earth has become. And, after the initial shock, I think he truly believed that even a solitary exile was preferable to living in the dehumanized vacuum that Earth is becoming. He left your mind free, both of the dogmas of the Instrumentality and of his own beliefs and prejudices. Few parents have achieved such an enlightened goal. You can be proud."

"And she will be exhausted," boomed Kli from the doorway, "if she does not eat something substantial and sleep for a good many hours. You forget, Alice, that we who are still incarnate have needs that never trouble you."

"True," answered the Companion sadly. "I always loved the sound of my own voice, and now that that is all I have left of myself, I tend to overuse it. Pardon me, child. Go with Kli and refresh yourself."

Ila laid a tender hand on the black case. "Having you with me is almost like having my father, Alice. You remind me of him." Then she went to Kli, who scooped her up and sailed away with her, down the well to the lower level where food was prepared and served.

Alice, left alone and still switched on, sat on the small table that had been placed for her and her toplight flashed with activity. Around her, there was a shimmer in the air, as if something that was all but invisible moved. Vlin, watching from an inner doorway from which she had just emerged, smiled.

"The gods have their own ways," she murmured to herself, then turned and went downward by another way.

CHAPTER EIGHTEEN

The crèche-ship orbited a ruined and uninhabited planet. The first thing that Dor could remember actually realizing was the fact that no one in all the Universe knew or cared about the ship. He lay in his sleep-capsule, thinking of the shattered landscape below, onto which he had been dumped several times to live or to die, as luck would have it. Being the steady creature he was, he had survived circumstances that had been fatal to many of his more imaginative companions. He woke often, though, with cold sweat soaking his bedclothes.

Only he, of all the children he knew or had heard of, had been planeted four times. It was as if the Assessor were doubtful of him, unsure that he was not more than he seemed. At the age of eight, the boy had assessed himself even more thoroughly than had the Assessor. He was obscurely ashamed that he had survived when many whom he had considered far more worthy of life had died. He knew himself to be slow and deliberate in his thinking, though not in his physical reflexes. He had no flair for anything, even weaponry. He felt himself inferior and thought that that was the reason for the repeated testing of his abilities.

It had never occurred to him that the Assessor, perfect complex of computer that it was, might be paranoid. It had never occurred to anyone, human or Servo, to question the decisions of their topmost authority. And none knew, now, that that authority had been designed, programmed and imprinted with all his own quirks by Valens Ward, one of the original designers of the crèche system. Whose tenth wife had plotted his downfall and had been exposed just in time. Her name was Dora.

The random consonant-vowel-consonant combination that the naming-mechanism had burdened Dor with had brought with it a kind of training that no other of the children ever reared in the crèche-ship had known. Lying in his capsule, dreamily assimilating the specifications for the air recycler of a scout ship, the boy drifted between sleep and dim awareness, knowing that, if he survived, he would probably be assigned to one of those probes whose purpose was to determine the coordinates of points in distant systems. He didn't feel the subtle change of pressure in the capsule when its seal-tight cover clamped quietly into place. He didn't miss the faint stirrings and murmurings of the ship, for his head was filled with the precise voice of the auto-teacher.

He did note immediately the disappearance of the hiss of oxygen into his shell. He sat upright and his head thumped into the transparent seal above him. He tore the electrodes from his head impatiently and strained against the cover, but it was hermetically sealed against the chance of air loss in the ship. And its oxygen intake was silent, still.

Dor lay back, slowly and carefully. He knew that any exertion would simply exhaust his small supply of air, so he let himself go limp, stilled the frantic claustrophobia that made him want to claw and to scream and to tear at the walls of the capsule. But the boy was tough . . . his unreasonably stern training had, most unintentionally, developed his natural capacities far beyond their normal scope. He had self-control that most human beings hadn't developed at forty. He lay quiet, rationing his breath, inhaling only when his lungs strained against his control and red streaks shot across his vision.

The Nans checked every capsule, when it was occupied, at ten-minute intervals. Dor knew that he must stretch his two minutes' worth of air into at most eight minutes. Possibly not more than four or five. He had been in such a dreamy state at the last check that he had little idea how long ago it had been.

The capsule was programmed to trigger a complex of signals when its inhabitant suffered any sort of physical stress. But its programming had been overridden, evidently, by a direct command from the Assessor. Dor lay in his capsule, sipping air with stringent economy, and realized in a combination of intuition and logic that the Assessor was deliberately and coldly doing its best to eliminate him.

His slow brain accepted the fact without surprise. He had never felt himself to be important in any way, and the only facet of the problem that puzzled him was the reason. He made no trouble, and he had done what was required of him adequately, if not more. He mulled and mulled, but it would not come clear. Then the stubbornness that complemented his toughness came to his aid.

I don't know *why*, he thought, as the air seemed to swell hotly in his chest, "but I'm no worse than a lot of the others. I'm not going to die just because the Assessor wants me to. He'll have to kill me."

The minutes dragged by, spanning eons of subjective time. At last, the startled face of a Nan appeared above the capsule and began unsealing it with great speed. Dor released the last hoarded breath he had gleaned from the depleted supply, then drew a great, deep lungful of ship's air. It was laden with metallic and antiseptic odors and had been recycled more than a few times, but it was glorious.

Several Nans were now clustered about Dor's capsule. They were communicating in their own code of twittering beeps, but Dor knew that they were sorting out all the possible malfunctions that might have occurred. He smiled to himself. They would never find the right one, he knew, for they were themselves only machines and never questioned the super-machine that directed all their activities.

Revived, the boy sat up and clambered out of the thing that had so nearly become his coffin. One of the Nans helped him down and led him away to the diagnostic machine for a checkup. He went docilely and stood quietly as the many-armed "doctor" went over him. When the tell-tale pronounced him fit, he was led away to the refectory and fed an extra ration of nutri-broth, which he found to be no great treat.

At last, they let him be, and he wandered into the common-room, where most of the juveniles between the ages of six and twelve gathered between training session. Dor wandered among them, watching their motions, listening to their talk, wondering what made him so different that he would be singled out for such a strange fate. He well knew that the Assessor could order his brain removed for use in a cyber-mechanism at any time that tests determined him suitable for such use. Why, then, such a roundabout way of getting rid of him?

The boy, square and stocky in his jumpsuit, stopped in the midst of the chattering throng of children. He nodded, slowly, turned, and left the room. The hallway was empty except for the figure of a Nan, just rounding the curve that followed the outer hull of the ship. Dor squared his shoulders and scurried for the cross-hall that led to the Assessor.

The doorway that led into the body of the Assessor was dark, but his presence caused a wall lamp to pulse into brightness. The dark screen where the face of the Assessor normally was to be seen began to glow, and that benign countenance took shape there.

"Well, now," it began in its usual grandfatherly

tones, "is there some sort of emergency? Where is your Nan? Come, child, tell me your name."

Dor looked it in the eyes and said, "I am Dor. You've never seen me before, but you've been trying to get rid of me ever since I can remember. You just now tried to smother me in my capsule. I came to tell you that you might as well kill me the usual way . . . I'm not going to die on my own, just to please you."

The Assessor hummed agitatedly for a mini-second. The face it showed to the world dissolved into scrambled lines for a moment, as it chattered, "But that won't do! The tests won't allow it. And I'm programmed to obey the tests! You must . . . you must . . . you must . . ." And then the screen was shot with wild lines of light, the hum became frantic, there was a terrible spatter of sparks from several components, and the light went out.

Dor stood there for a stunned instant, then he realized that he must run for cover. There was never anyone in this corridor leading to the Assessor, and the cross-corridor had been dimmed for sleeping-span. The boy ghosted along the twilit passages and gained the dubious safety of his capsule without being seen by human or Nan or even Servo.

From that refuge, he heard the first querulous beep when a capsule, trying to relay some abnormality to the Assessor, found itself unable to complete the circuit. After a short time a much louder alarm began to hoot in the depths of the ship. A bustle of Nans and human attendants clanked and shuffled away in the direction of the primary computer, to return, a bit later, clattering and buzzing with alarm.

Safe in his capsule, Dor began to smile. He felt certain that the Assessor was dead . . . its circuits scrambled and shorted. And he had done it, Dor the slow-witted butt of its deadly jokes. He turned on his side and slipped the electrodes onto his skull. He would need it all, to make a scout ship man.

CHAPTER NINETEEN

Again Ila woke to see the tank moving slowly upward. She moved her hand to her head, and her fingers brushed a feathery hand that was busy removing the wiring from her. Alice, beside her, was flashing her toplight impatiently. Ila yawned and sat up.

"I think I'm back again," she said to the Companion. "What is it, Alice?"

"If an eight-year-old—a not-too-bright eight-year-old—can bollix up an Assessor until it blows its circuits, there may still be hope for the human race, Ila. Everything that has been tried for bringing the Instrumentality down has aimed at changing the legalities by which it was installed. But if enough dissidents defied individual computers, particularly if there are many computers imprinted with flawed personalities, it could bring the thing to a halt purely because there wouldn't be enough of them left to run things. We'd win by default!"

"It could be that you're right," the girl agreed. "But we are here—and we don't even know where here is, with reference to Earth—and it is all there. How could we ever get the idea back to the people involved?"

"Have you forgotten that the Vla have instant matter transfer, too?" Alice snorted. "We could go back, ourselves, and tell them."

"Have you forgotten how tightly controlled it is back there?" asked Ila. "The instant I reappeared on Earth, I'd be grabbed, run through a succession of Sifters, and there wouldn't be enough left of me to fertilize a rose bush. We can't go back in person, Alice. But there just might be a way. The gods said they could see Earth . . . even communicate with some people there. They don't any more, because their communicants get put into madhouses. I wonder if they couldn't reach children, though?"

Alice made a sound between a burble and a hiccup. "Now that's an idea to work with. If enough of the crèche children found that they could deceive and even destroy the Assessors, not to mention the Nans, there would be a full-scale revolution, right there. And if the children left on Earth were taught the same things to try on their monitors and autoteachers . . . even," sadly, "their Companions, they would all but finish the job."

"Vlin said we'd have more chances to face the gods," Ila replied. "Work it out in as fine detail as you can, Alice. We'll see what they think of it. If it should work, I'd go to my grave a happy woman, knowing that if the Instrumentality hadn't 'protected' itself by exiling me, it wouldn't have connived at its own downfall."

Kli, Vleer, and Vlin had been listening to the exchange with great interest. Vleer now stretched his wings wide and lifted himself a few inches from the floor. Ila could now see that his eye-corners were twitching with delight, as were those of the other two Vla, who also lifted to join the elder in a tiptoe saraband about Ila's chair.

They sang softly as they danced, spinning silently in a circle of white wings. The whirling figures became a blur of humming sound and feathery motion, and Ila thought dreamily of old tales of enchanted spinning wheels (whatever they might have been).

A sound beside her made her turn her head to see Hla settling her wings and preening her face feathers. The young Vlammalba bent to touch Ila's cheek with her wing tip and said, "You have pleased the Old Ones. I have never seen any of the elders in a Dance of Delight, for, though there has been much joy in our existence, only a unique and exquisite thing moves them to perform it."

The two sat quietly, watching the lovely patterns the elder Vla made, until the dance came to an end and the three settled again to the floor and looked at Ila. Vlin moved her hands in the graceful movement of acceptance and happiness and sang, "It is seldom that we are allowed to see the intricate workings of the gods moving into the affairs of beings who still inhabit flesh. We were told, there at the High Place of Union, that such a working-out of fate was being made manifest in our time, but we, long used to a certain sameness in our lives, had no comprehension of the loveliness that meant."

Kli's basso boomed out, "To be instruments of the gods is a wonderful thing. If, thereby, you free the very young of a sentient race from cruelty and terror, oh, that is joy, indeed!"

"But they are not yet free," Ila said sadly. "Who knows if they ever will be?"

"Of what else could the gods have spoken, there on the pinnacle of the world?" asked Vleer. "Our own troubles are small, in comparison. Only the deaths of Ered are great in the affairs of Vlahil. But the torture and deaths of children, feathered or no, is a thing of such moment that the stars shudder and the fabric of time is rent. So said the gods. So we say, Vlammalba, Vlammere, Ered, and all."

"And those two poor babes, there in the south," mourned Vlin, "are so greatly the victims of terrible error that their own crimes against life are understandable. We will cure them, all of us together, of their fears and their doubts. Then they will be whole and free, and they are made of such stuff that greatness is possible to both.

"But there is even greater need than theirs. There is a third entity there, very small as yet. For they will have a youngling of their own, in no very long time. That small one will be warped and twisted by its parents' fears, if they are not healed. Your work is very fruitful, Ila, for their memories, passed through your more mature mind that is also one accessible to us, give us the keys to their cure."

"More is needed," said Alice firmly. "You must go, at least once more, into their remembrances. So, as I have been reminded in the past, you need both rest and food, Ila. Go, now, and get both, and I will sit here and put things into clear order."

When the other had left, Alice sat in the stillness, her toplight busy, her interior rippling with electronic motion, and, again, there was a shimmer about her, as though invisible spectators were examining her molecular ruminations and subatomic recordings.

CHAPTER TWENTY

The selection tunnel was a place of chill metal and gray plastics. Dor glanced behind him at the line of shivering candidates and wondered how he had had the temerity to hope for a scout ship assignment. His one moment of triumph was so far in the past that it seemed as if he must have dreamed it. The giddy warmth of that victory, it is true, had enabled him to attack the difficulties of his training with tenacity and to conquer most of them, but now he stood, nude and forlorn, among many. Why should the computers choose him?

There was a short, stocky girl just in front of him, and he noticed that she was trembling even more than he was; he could even hear the faint click of her teeth as they chattered. Her skin had attained a strange shade, its natural creamy brown drawn up into goose pimples that were almost purplish with the cold of the tunnel. The violet-hued lighting that made all look either ill or long-dead added to her oddness.

On impulse, he reached forward and touched her arm. She whipped about, and he saw a pointed face that seemed to be all big, black, flashing eyes.

"Are you afraid?" he whispered, darting a wary glance at the monitor on the wall just beyond them.

She tightened her lips over her teeth for an instant, then she smiled, and, for a short moment, he saw another person, brave and free, glint behind her eyes. Then she said, "Yes, I suppose I am. I'm Jir . . . who are you?"

"Dor," he replied. "I don't really expect to be selected. There are so many, and most of them are better scouts than I am. But I'm glad I'm here. I tried my best, anyway."

Jir looked up at him and opened her lips to speak, but at that precise instant the wide door to their right slid open with a hiss, and a metallic voice said, "Two—enter!"

The unexpectedness of it made Dor give a gasp, but there was no doubt . . . the door was open and he and Jir were the only two within its range. As one, they reached out and clasped their hands together, then they stepped into the bare cubicle and heard the door zip shut behind them.

Immediately, a row of lights was activated. Knowing the ways of their inhuman environment well, the two moved forward to stand with their feet on the sensors, which instantly identified them from footprints, body chemistry, and weight. Then panels opened on all sides and the multitudinous tubes, arms, and paraphernalia of the selector began their work. Lights flickered continuously, and there was a deep thrumming from the walls.

The two youngsters stood patiently, enduring the

indignities to which they were so well accustomed. Once, Dor looked at Jir and shrugged; once, Jir looked at Dor and grinned. Both felt a wild excitement in the pits of their stomachs, for they knew that those rejected out of hand were not called into the selector.

Reams of data were fed into the central computer system. Electrical impulses danced madly through the banks, recording everything that might possibly be of importance concerning the two candidates. The solar-powered electrical plant handled that and numerous other demands without effort, drawing on its inexhaustible supplier, the sun. And the effect of a terrific pulse of energy, caused by a solar flare, arrived and, for one micro-second, boosted the electrical input to the computer by the tiniest possible fraction.

A molecule was shifted microscopically from position. One small but important fact was changed as it went into the irrevocable maw of the central computer. Jir was listed as a male. The intricate orders, being cut simultaneously with the arrival of the data, therefore listed two males as the complement of personnel on the L-210 scout ship.

Supply orders, also going out simultaneously, listed cold-sleep gear, resuscitation equipment, weaponry for both long- and short-range use, clothing, food concentrates, auto-doctor (with appropriate medical supplies), and the infinite array of minor necessities for keeping both ship and crew in operating condition. However, two most important things were omitted from the list. There was no meteor deflector ordered (it had been determined that, on a cost-benefit basis, it was cheaper to lose the one-in-ten-thousand ship than to install deflectors in all of them). And no contraceptives were added to the water-purifying system. Both deletions were to have major impact on Dor and Jir.

When the selector had completed its task, a panel opened on each side of the room and a tray slid out of each. On the trays were clear-seal-wrapped bundles that opened to reveal the ugly gray shipsuits of the scout service. Their shoulder bands blazed with red zigzag lines. Dor thought he had never seen anything so beautiful.

Without wasting time, the two zipped themselves into the suits. As soon as the last seal was closed and the soft footgear was donned, another door whispered open at the back of the selector. A Servo stood there, and it immediately conducted them to a lift. Less than an hour from the moment when they entered the door, Dor and Jir were lying down in cold-sleep capsules, watching Servos make connections, tighten fittings on tubing, and activate the mechanisms that would—or would not—maintain their status as living beings in the months or years ahead.

A voice whose source they could not see said, "You are assigned to scout Area R^{10} of Quadrant Ss 1417. Your ship will be launched in ten hours, by which time you will be in cold sleep. Resuscitation will be activated by arrival in the assigned quadrant.

Orders are contained in the ship's computer, which will guide your exploration. Serve the Instrumentality well. There is need of the information you will provide."

Then the seals were placed over their tense faces and the dark wall of sleep came down and blotted out everything.

Jir felt all over as if she were a foot that had gone to sleep. Tingling numbness became exquisite agony as nerves returned to life and muscles began to jerk spasmodically. She opened her eyes, but there was only a blur for what seemed a very long time. She could hear swishings and gurglings in the walls of her cold-sleep container, together with a steady *ping! ping!* that could only be a monitor informing the ship's computer that she was waking on schedule.

She was one large mass of pain, now. Her forehead throbbed, her entire body throbbed with the newly resumed beating of her heart. She grew terribly warm, then wickedly cold, by turns. It seemed that the resuscitation would never end and release her from its torture. But it was done, at last.

With a sigh, the seal above her opened, and the surface beneath her head and shoulders rose, lifting her smoothly into a sitting position. Turning her head for the first time in an unmeasured infinity, she saw Dor also sitting and beginning to stretch. She opened her mouth and found that her jaws were as stiff as though they had rusted, and her tongue seemed made of old sacking. An apparatus swung in an arc, coming to rest convenient to her mouth, and she took its nipple in her mouth and felt the grateful coolness of water.

Neither ever remembered how long it took to gather enough strength and mobility to climb from the capsules, but it was accomplished at last. They clung together for a time, trying to find their balance in the weak ship's gravity. Then, true to their long conditioning, they consulted the computer.

They received a complete printout, including all that had happened since they walked through the door of the selector. In that printout was a record of the pulsation of the electrical supply, the error in the data, the assignment of the mission, length of journey (four and a half years, by the chronometer; an incomprehensible span of distance), and the exact time of entry into Quadrant Ss 1417.

With the impetus of familiar routine to spur them on, the scouts activated the proper sequences of programs, noted the data given by the scanners, and allowed themselves to punch the food-delivery buttons. Sitting in their tailored spaces, they leaned back their heads and allowed the warm sustenance to slide down their throats. It even had flavor, something new to both, as crèche food was nutritious and tasteless in the extreme. Subjectively, they had just met, had only in the past hour realized that they were actually to be scouts.

Now, the actuality of their situation began to become real to them. The knowledge that they were

totally beyond the reach of the Instrumentality left
both somewhat staggered. Only the relatively pow-
erless computer of the ship represented the terrible
potency of the computerized government. The idea
was intoxicating.

Yet neither young Terran had ever been allowed
to entertain the notion of self-determination. It did
not occur to either to wrench control of the ship
from the computer and to head for the nearest
planet, to live on their own for the rest of their lives.
The one thing that the Instrumentality taught thoroughly and well was fear of authority, coupled with
terror of the unknown. And Jir and Dor had been
taught uniquely personal terrors of their own.

Still, as days and weeks passed, they grew
strangely contented with their routine tasks, their
increasingly satisfying talks before time for sleep.
The reality of near autonomy was creeping into
their habits, but neither knew it. They merely knew
that they had never dreamed that the life of a scout
could possibly be so much more wonderful than
that of a crèche-child.

Their first planetfall was dull. In their self-con-
tained suits, they left the scout ship to wander for a
short time across a desert of finely ground sand that
the thin air moved restlessly about their ankles.
They took samples of the sand and of occasional
rocks, but there was nothing else, though they faith-
fully divided the expanse of the lifeless world into
sectors and touched down on each one.

The second, third, fourth . . . and many more

. . . were semi-arid, with sparse and primitive vegetation. Only one held mobile life, and that was on a level comparable to amoeba. But it was fun, though neither knew the word, to wander about places that were free of a moil of contemporaries, Nans, and Servos. And the notion was gradually borne into their minds that there was a great deal of space to which the Instrumentality was irrelevant.

The meteor came as a shocking surprise. They had grown used to the sharp pings of small fragments upon the skin of the ship, and familiarity had bred a false sense of security. But the system into which they moved was thick with debris from some long-past planetary catastrophe, and when a chunk a third the mass of the ship collided with them, they were taken by surprise. The automatic sealers were independent of the computer, which saved their lives. For the meteor ripped into the hull on the side containing it and shattered the mechanical brain past any hope of repair.

All the programs were obliterated. The careful instructions that were to guide them disappeared in powder and ash. Only Dor's painstaking method of learning everything about his craft that was there to be learned allowed them to locate a suitable world and to land there without disaster.

When the hatch cycled open, they peered out cautiously, huddling into the security of their suits and fingering their weapons. Spindly trees grew on all sides of the clearing where Dor had set them down.

With growing alarm, they realized that the forest was alive with living creatures.

"Any beast encountered is potentially dangerous," Jir muttered under her breath. "Take no chance; shoot to kill." She began to tremble, and suddenly she was again four years old, huddled against a cold dome, surrounded by unknown dangers. She raised the laser rifle and fired into the top of a tree.

She hit nothing, but the hum of busy life that had filled the wood was hushed immediately. Behind her, Dor had also begun to shake.

"We're trapped here," he whispered. "We'll never be able to lift the ship again, damaged as it is. Those things out there only have to wait. Without the computer, the food-delivery won't work. We've got to go out there and kill animals for food. They taught us how, when they planeted us, but I never thought I'd have to do it."

Their first expedition was hell. There was no bush or tree without its burden of deadly living things. Knowing that they couldn't kill all, they tried only to destroy those creatures that were large enough to be an immediate danger, or those that might be eaten. The slaying of the first Ered was a matter of blind panic.

The light-dark cycle arbitrarily imposed on the various crèches was considerably shorter than that of Vlahil, and the two computer-reared children were as inflexible, in their own way, as those machines that had taught them. Night caught them still in the forest, and the Ered, walking quietly along its path in the moonlight, met them face to face. The gentle touch of the creature's calming thought was lost amid the scarlet moil of terror in Jir's mind. Her conditioning held, and the Ered died.

The weeks in the forest had disoriented the scouts . . . had, in fact, driven them almost over the edge into insanity. And, though they had no way of knowing it, their inner chaos was transmitted on an empathic level to the beasts nearby, spreading outward from them in a ripple effect until much of the area was in the grip of unreasoning ferocity. So, when the Ered at last sent the Terrans into sleep, most of the creatures in the forest dropped into an almost catatonic state, recovering from that mad period of violence.

When Dor and Jir awoke to find themselves invisibly imprisoned in the clearing, they were frantically disturbed. But fruit and grainy bread appeared in their clearing each morning. No creature moved within sight in the trees they could see. Nothing threatened them in any way. They calmed, bit by bit, the ruptured order of their minds settling into something resembling patterned thought and behavior.

So, for weeks that grew into months, they were given time to think, as the Ered far in the north worked to smooth their emotions into calmness.

CHAPTER TWENTY-ONE

While those months fled by, Ila and Alice were busy.
There was much for Ila to learn, much for Alice to
teach, and the Vla and the Ered both taught and
learned in constant interaction with the two.

Ila had moved, at her invitation, into the Oldest
Ered's habitation. "You will be nearer to Rhoosh
here, and we will be able to work closely without my
being forced to travel. At my age, travel is wearing
and diminishes my effectiveness," the Oldest had
whispered into Ila's mind, and the girl had gratefully accepted her offer.

Alice had contributed her services in a crash program that rendered the Vla language accessible to
the girl on every level that held common terms.
Then the Vla had borne her away to Rhoosh, where
she began pouring into their recording devices the
infinity of information, poetry, music, and personal
observations held by her unique amalgam of hu-
manity and computer.

The spring wore away, and summer came. Ila noticed that when Hliss or Hler visited her with the
elders, they were absentminded and abstracted. She
mentioned this to Vleer, and the old Vlammere
twitched his eye-corners.

"Have you forgotten? We draw near to the time of the mating flights. This time will be their first, and we expect little of use from them for weeks before and after. For this reason, we elders dread the approach of midsummer. But ah! it was different when we were of an age to ride the thermals with our mates. Well do I remember my first meeting with Vlin, though it was a hundred seasons ago. So intense was our joy in one another that the Universe disappeared and nothing was left but two intoxicated selves.

"And yet"—the old Vlammere sighed a minor note—"it is better now. Vlin and I can communicate without song or motion. We understand one another as totally as separate beings may. We can associate without loss of judgment. I greatly fear our younglings are in error when they desire to unite our divided race in permanent closeness. I fear that it will weaken the concentration of our varying works and calculations."

Ila asked, "How long have the young ones been taken up with this idea, Vleer? Has it been for several years . . . or is it only for the past few months?"

The Vlammere looked at her intently. "Only a short while. Since, perhaps, your fellow beings came to Vlahil. Might that be the source of the unrest?"

"I don't say that it is," she answered, "but it was shortly after their landing here that the two of them discovered the comfort they could find in sexual closeness. They are so very young . . . their intoxication was well-nigh Vla in its intensity. And the Oldest Ered tells me that they broadcast with terrific strength on a subliminal level of emotion. It could be that they are the source and the fountain of the problem among your own young. We may know the truth easily . . . if the Vla no longer are obsessed by their project after the Terrans are removed from this continent, we may be sure that was its cause."

"So the gods gave you their counsel also?" sang Vleer.

"They told me that I must go with them," Ila said sadly. "You will transfer them to the wild continent, where there are no Ered, and I will go with them, for my form is the same as theirs and I will cause them no terror. And I will teach them the things that I'm learning now, from you and Vlin and Kli and the Oldest Ered. But it is hard. I have come to feel that you are my own people, and I love you." Her eyes filled with tears, and Vleer touched her cheek with a wing tip.

"Oh, child, have no grief! We will not abandon you. The transfer works in both directions, once we have sent across the base key. You will visit us and we you, and when your task is done, the three of you will return to this side of the sea to live among us. But there will, of course, be four of you by that time. What a fascinating thing it will be to watch the development of one of your kind from infancy!"

Ila brightened, and the voice of the Oldest Ered rustled in her mind, "You will have, before you go, a wonderful thing given you. The Vla have decided that you will go with them to the Ancient Place, where not even the Ered have ever gone. You will share the music and the rising-of-hearts, and you will witness the mating flights. They know that you, too, have mated, and that you have lost him who shared your life. Once more, they will that you may share the tenderness of that time.

"You will also have a companion—other than Alice. My child-in-heart, who will one day take my place among our people, has volunteered to go with you. She wishes to try her training upon the truly untaught creatures of that wild place. She also believes that she will be able to reinforce your strength in teaching those entrusted to your care. And you will, I know, find it less and less difficult to understand one another, though she has not, as yet, learned to speak into the mind."

There was a moment when all their minds were washed in a haze of violet. An answering tone of pale pink came from the Oldest Ered, and another Ered entered the chamber from the anteroom. Though she made no sound in their minds, Ila and Vleer saw clearly a sequence of pictures moving there. The young Ered before them held Ila's hand, as they both went into a thick forest, followed by Dor and Jir.

Ila rose and held out her hand to the young one. "I'm so happy that you decided to come with me," she said. "We will soon come to know and to love one another."

The Ered nodded, then pictured herself with another of her kind, arms linked, heads together, surrounded by the creamy hue of questioning.

"You want to take along your mate!" Ila said with certainty. "And I wouldn't have you leave him behind at all."

Another Ered came from the anteroom, and Ila was overjoyed to find that he was her own original Ered. She greeted him with pats on the shoulder, then turned a beaming face to Vleer and the Oldest. "I think I'm beginning to realize how your world is shaped by the gods. They taught the Ered—right?— who taught the Vla. Both learned the value of kindness and generosity and love for living things. And that made your world the place it is, willing to go to a lot of trouble for two castaway children from an alien world."

There was a time of silence, while all there considered future problems and plans, and at its end Vleer said to Ila, "We make ready, now, to go to the Ancient Place. Hliss will carry you to Rhoosh, and we will leave with tomorrow's dawn. At the end of the mating flights, we will bear you and Alice to Rhooshal, where we will be met by your four companions. You will all go through the transfer to the wild continent. So make your farewells to the Oldest. It will be long before you see her again."

With some sadness, Ila touched her cheek to that of the Oldest and felt that hard little hand patting her back.

"Go to joy, child, and then to useful work. Not even the gods can know greater satisfaction than can

be yours. I will wait for your return, for I must see
you again, as well as that wonderful child that you
will bring back with you, before I go out of this
cumbersome flesh into the freedom beyond."

There was a pause, then the dry voice whispered
again, "And do not forget, whatever you do, that
Alice has brought us music and you have brought us
dance. We must dance again together, to music the
Ered will make with the instruments Alice showed
us how to make and to play. Await that time with
happiness."

They flew away into a twilit sky, and Ila felt a
strange and joyful wistfulness, as though she were
leaving behind her own unremembered mother.

CHAPTER TWENTY-TWO

The Ancient Place was not among those needled peaks beyond which lay the High Place of Union. When the Vlammere from Rhoosh set out in the dawn light, Ila realized very soon that they were flying northward, along the river. As they flew, they sang . . . a different song, the girl realized, from that lovely strain with which she had been awakened during her stays at Rhoosh and Rhooshal. This was a bubbling melody that flowed, in its way, like the river below.

Hliss sang, as he carried her, and the vibrant boom of his deep baritone vibrated his bones and her own. About them, the variations in tonalities soared and skipped and quivered with tremolos. The song never ended, but it altered with each hour of flight, and there came a moment when Ila knew that she was hearing other, lighter voices that gained in volume as they drew nearer. Soon, those from Rhooshal were flying among their brother-mates, and the music became unutterably, piercingly sweet, touched with tenderness and anticipation.

About the Vla swooped and darted a host of the dancing birds, adding their undisciplined trills to the mating song. Ila found Vlin flying beside Hliss, and she pointed to the birds and asked, "Are they going, too?"

"Only a part of the way," Vlin crooned. "They are our far-distant cousins, those who chose the way of instinct instead of the thorny path of will. Yet they rejoice with us at the time of the mating flights, and we delight in them, for they remind us of the things we lost and the things we gained when we accepted the harder way."

So they flew through the early sunlight, in the winy air of midsummer, with the scents of greenery and blossoms and the water-and-stone smell of the river below flowing about them as they went. The nature of the land changed, the stone of the cliff at river's edge receded and disappeared, the meadows spread in flower-spangled lushness to the horizon on the east and a forest on the west. And when they reached a point where the waters of the river became deep and swift and green, the Vla veered away toward the beckoning forest.

Then Ila saw that there were other groups in the sky, some so distant as to be mere specks. The music grew in volume, coming now from all points of the compass. The growing mass of Vla sped toward the trees, and the Terran now was able to see that they were immense ones with towering crests and a greater spread of branches than she had seen on any other trees on Vlahil. Beyond the trees there seemed to be a large hill or small mountain that caught the sunlight and was fogged in a haze of gold.

Over the leading hem of the forest the multitude flew, making for that golden hill. When the first-comers reached the inner ring of trees that circled it, they came gently to a landing and busied themselves immediately with gathering blooms and binding them into garlands, weaving vines and branches into bowers about smaller trees. They worked two by two, and Ila knew that this must be the first step in the courtship that led to the final joy of the mating flights.

When all the Vla had arrived, the forest edge was aswirl with motion. Some built their bowers high in towering trees, some upon the ground, and some incorporated flowering shrubs into their architecture.

Those who were not involved in the proceedings gathered on the crest of the hill, the oldest and the youngest all together, to stand, wings wafting gently to bear most of their weight, singing and singing as if their spirits were trying to find freedom through their pulsing throats. There was constant change among their ranks, some arriving and some leaving, but the volume of their song never diminished.

Ila sat in a maze of enchantment, leaning against a mossy stone. She didn't even miss Alice, who had been left behind with the Oldest Ered. The air about her shimmered with music, the forest before her shimmered with winged forms and floating banners of blossom. Such beauty she had never known before, and the day sank into twilight before she roused from her bemusement.

Then she realized that many of the old and the young had been busy themselves, gathering and preparing a banquet of fruits and crushed grains and the tantalizing herbal broths she had found so satisfying. As the joyful young left the bower-building, their elders called them to the evening meal, and when darkness was fully over the forest, all were sitting or standing or reclining about the array of food.

Bulbous torches lit the scene, and Ila, examining one, found the spherical glow to be a stone of strange crystal, whose light seemed to originate deep within it. There was a diamond-hard brilliance to the light thus given that lent a fairylike unreality to the tall shapes of the Vla, the brightness of the many-colored fruits, and the greenness of leaf and grass that edged the fantastic spectacle.

The music and the feast ended at last, and the torches were dimmed to glimmers. Ila rested in a mound of ferny plants that lent a spicy scent to her dreams, and the night passed in a tranquil succession of deep sleep and happy musings.

Morning found a much different atmosphere from that bustle of the evening before. Bowers completed, the marriage meal done, the high music sung, the Vla prepared for the rising-of-hearts. Vlin showed Ila to a shaded spot at the edge of the forest, then the tall Vlammalba joined her fellows in a great circle that completely girdled the hill. All stood tall, heads thrown back, wings spread wide to catch the faint morning breeze.

There was a long moment of silence, of waiting, and then a lone voice was raised from the far side of the hill, to be joined in a descending scale by other voices, one by one, until a single sustained note of harmony crowned the eminence. It was held for two heartbeats, then was cut short, leaving a hollow space in the air where it had hung.

Vleer's voice rose then, a deep basso, seeming to be rooted in the deeps of the mountains, to be joined in the ascending scale until the note hung, again, in the enchanted air. And on this note, the circle of Vla began to rise, borne up by controlled sweeps of their wings, holding perfectly their positions relative to the hill and to one another.

Again the note was scythed short, and the rising of winged bodies stopped. Now all the voices of the Vlammere sang, an organ-note so deep that it seemed to shake the leaves above Ila. They were answered by the Vlammalba, whose strong sopranos rang in a triumphant trumpet-note above the multitudinous hum of their deeper-voiced companions.

Now began the true rising-of-hearts. The voices asked and answered, building a fugue of melody and countermelody containing the first true counterpoint Ila had heard in the music of the Vla. And with the rising joy and excitement of the music, the bodies of the singers also rose, higher and higher into the morning sky, until they wreathed an invisible cone projected upward from the base of the hill.

The rising sun warmed the shapes with rose and gold, and as it climbed the sky, first one and then another of the feathery beings dropped from its position to spiral downward with the airy reluctance of a single fluff of down. Soon the sky was full of them, dropping like a strange snow to touch lightly down upon the hill below. When all were again upon their toes instead of their wings, the music died away as voice after voice was silenced. There was a pause, relaxed now, almost dreamy, as the sun struck downward over the treetops onto the soil of the clearing about the hill.

As if newly awakened, the Vla stretched and turned to prepare food for the morning meal. Ila rose to help them, but her heart was still full of the sight and the sound and the glory of the rising-of-hearts, and she knew she would never see anything so lovely again.

The morning drifted by like a dream. Pairs of young Vla drifted through the wood and about the hill, pausing now and again to touch wing tips or to place palm to palm. Ila saw Hla and Hliss moving about a low-hung bower, touching the waxy blossoms woven into its walls. She smiled as they passed her, but they knew only each other and passed without their customary greeting. The girl realized that the older Vla had not exaggerated . . . the Vla, when mating, lived in a state of almost disembodied intoxication. The world about them, the tasks and ideas that enthralled them in their own places and times, had disappeared as if they had never been.

Midday passed, but there was no communal meal. The elders and the young withdrew into the deeps of the wood to rest, perching on convenient branches until the forest seemed to have been visited by an unseasonable snowfall. Ila napped beneath a tremendous bole that towered above her, spreading its branches to shut out not only the sun but almost the light of day itself.

But when evening drew on, there was a stirring among the resting Vla. Vlin woke Ila and led her back to the clearing about the hill, where they found the mating pairs waiting, palm-to-palm, for their arrival. The torches were brought forth and stimulated to their maximum glow, and one of the lights was given to each couple on the hill. As the sun sank behind the horizon and the light of day dimmed, Hla and Hliss raised their torch and lifted their wings. A sigh moved among the elders and the very young like the rustle of breeze among leaves.

With no sound, no song, only a tenderness that was almost audible, the two rose with short, powerful strokes of their wings, their faces close, the rosy organs on their breasts pulsing, drawing nearer and nearer one to the other until Ila could see the flowerlike organs join together, petal overlapping petal, as the new mates moved upward. As if their ascent had been a signal, other pairs began to rise, their torches adding to the numbers of the stars until the sky was studded with twinkling will-o'-the-wisps.

So gentle had been the moment, so reverent the mood, that Ila only belatedly realized that she had beheld the actual consummation of the Vla mating. Her eyes filled with tears as she remembered the lost tenderness of her own brief marriage. But she was roused from her thoughts by Vlin's touch upon her shoulder.

"We must go," said the Vlammalba. "They will return with the sun, and they will find food prepared with much love and understanding, but we will all be gone. They must have their weeks of union, as we who are older had and those who are younger will have, unless they choose to try another way of life that will destroy the need for the mating flights."

"It would be a tragedy to change it," said Ila, her mind still filled with the wonder of those soaring torches. "My world might have been much different had we been taught to separate ourselves, as you have done. Much suffering and cruelty might have been avoided, and many good minds might not have been wasted. I devoutly hope that taking away my charges will return the feelings of the young to the old patterns."

With little effort, the spectators laid out a feast for the returning mates, laid flowers among the fruits, and sang a quiet song of blessing. Then Kli lifted Ila and the entire group took wing, each aerie together, and flew away across the dark forest.

In the darkness it was hard to tell, but Ila knew that their number was growing smaller as the various aeries veered toward their own places. They winged through the night, with the stars winking distantly both above and below, reflected in the river.

Cradled against Kli's feathery chest, lulled by the steady *tha-da-dub* of his tripartite heart, the girl slept, and her dreams were happy ones.

EPILOGUE

The jungle whispered with stealthy movements, mold shifting minimally beneath quiet paws, leaves and twigs moving with small rustles at the passage of furred and leather-hided bodies. The hunters were out, stealthy beneath the dim moon of Vlahil, and the little beasts that knew themselves for prey were deep in their burrows or high in their nests.

The continent swept, wild and wide, in darkness from sea to sea. There was, however, one spot of light that marked the dwelling of reasoning beings.

Ila stood in the open door of her hut, transported in its entirety by the mechanisms of the Vla. The darkness that veiled the forest did not frighten her, for she felt the nearness of her Ered, the calming patterns of their minds overlaying the chaos of the untamed world in which they moved.

She turned to look into the hut. Dor and Jir sat at her table beneath the torch the Vla had provided for her use. They were reading, though the plates in their hands bore little resemblance to the books that had been Alice's lifetime's care. Alice sat on the table, her toplight flashing brilliantly. They had found that the Terrans responded far better to her teaching than to that of a fellow human being. Early conditioning was unquestionably a stubborn factor in the training of these children. But they were learning, Jir quickly and with bursts of intuitive insight, Dor with snaillike but retentive determination. Each week saw the person that Jir might one day become moving nearer and nearer to the surface of that interior tunnel into which she had been banished. Each month saw the deep distrust that hampered Dor in thought and action recede a bit into the past, to be replaced by interest in the new doors that were being cautiously opened to him.

Ila knew that she might wake any morning to hear the clear call of Vlin's or Kli's or Vleer's voice in the forest, calling her out for a day of joyful reunion or a brief journey back to Rhoosh or Rhooshal. Her exile was no burden, as she had feared, but a challenging task that she found more absorbing with each victory, more intriguing with each setback.

The Ered were her comfort and her enduring pleasure. The lumpy forms that were still frightening to Dor and Jir were familiar and dear to Ila. She observed with interest the gradual lessening of the hostility that had enwrapped the surrounding forest on their arrival. The two enigmatic little beings were slowly smoothing away the worst fears of the creatures nearby, working upon the actual fabric of their thought to change habits and to alter the direction of inborn instinct.

Predators were trying new foods, though they had no notion why they nibbled certain roots instead of pouncing upon a juicy Handmouse. Prey were learning new ways of moving through their world that would not tempt their old enemies into ingrained habits. Millennia hence, if Ered volunteered to continue the task, the wild continent might be akin to the world the Vla and the Ered knew.

And her own world, lost among the teeming galaxies, also might begin to hope. The gods had moved long steps ahead of the plan she and Alice had devised. Ila felt that many things, including her own exile to Vlahil, might well have been maneuvered by those trans-dimensional beings whose purposes and methods were beyond the comprehension of human, Ered, or Vla. There had even been a hint—no more than that—that the gods knew something of her lost love, who had been exiled long before she had.

Ila closed the door, and the light cast her sharp shadow against the wall. The ugly utilitarian hut had become home, inhabited by two children whom she had taken for her own, by Alice, who provided a warm link with her father, and by that small unknown whose presence became more obvious every day.

"Even the gods can't ask for more," Ila mused, patting Alice's case. She sat between Jir and Dor and lifted one of the ceramic plates the Vla had made to her order. Jir moved closer and touched her hand. Dor smiled shyly at her over his "book."

"Even the gods . . ."

ARDATH MAYHAR lives in the Attoyac River Bottoms of east Texas, where she raises goats, cows, chickens, turkeys, rabbits, and bees and writes books and stories. She had published a great deal of poetry, short fiction, and nonfiction before turning her hand to fantasy novels with *How the Gods Wove in Kyrannon*—and her reputation as a fantasy writer has been growing steadily ever since.